TRACES

FRAMED!

D0972915

With thanks to Sylvia for her generous gift of a surname for Olivia Pang

KINGFISHER
An imprint of Kingfisher Publications Plc
New Penderel House, 283-288 High Holborn
London WC1V 7HZ
www.kingfisherpub.com

This edition published by Kingfisher 2007
First published by Kingfisher 2005
2 4 6 8 10 9 7 5 3 1

A CIP catalogue record for this book
is available from the British Library.

ISBN 978 0 7534 1493 4

Printed in India
1TR/0307/THOM/(THOM)/80TORA/C

TRACES

FRAMED!

MALCOLM ROSE

KINGFISHER

ABOUT THE AUTHOR

Malcolm Rose, a former Senior Lecturer in Chemistry, is a well-known children's thriller writer of some 25 novels including five *Traces* titles. Malcolm has won the Angus Book Award and the Lancashire Book of the Year Award. His books regularly feature in the Book Trust 100 best books for children list. In the USA, *Traces: Framed!* was selected as a Best International Book by the International Reading Association. Malcolm lives in Sheffield.

Chapter One

The skeleton lay on the classroom floor and Luke Harding prowled around it, thinking. Then, on hands and knees, he went round again, taking a closer look. Still he didn't touch the specimen. Without looking up, he pointed to the ribcage and said, "Malc, there's a tiny nick on the sixth rib. Looks like a knife wound to me. Scan it, will you?"

The flattened orb moved in, hovered above the bleached bones and swept a laser over the fault. "It is consistent with a stab wound made by a narrow blade, pushed in at an approximate downward angle of forty-three degrees."

"From the lips of the cut, I'd say it was made on living bone and not done by cunning examiners on the skeleton. What do you think?"

"I do not have the capacity to think. I conduct forensic tests and supply facts. I confirm that the wound was inflicted on live bone by a sharp instrument with a slightly jagged edge."

Luke glanced over his shoulder at Malc. "What's it doing here?"

"Irrational question," the neutral male voice said.

"Well, what sort of exam is this?"

"Criminology, Year 11, Final Qualification, Advanced."

"Right," Luke replied with a grin. "Advanced. So what's a simple knife wound doing in an advanced exam? I'd have spotted it with my eyes closed."

"Illogical and unlikely."

"Oh, loosen up, Malc."

"This is your Final Qualification Examination. Not a time to be loose."

"You're seriously boring, you know. Anyway, let's do what I'm expected to do – and fail to get an answer, no doubt. A DNA scan, please."

Malc drifted down the entire length of the skeleton and then reported, "No traces left exposed."

"Hairs and fibres next."

"None detected."

Luke already knew that there would be no obvious traces to help him determine the victim's identity and the cause of death. Luke hadn't made it through to the top grade to have the answer handed to him on a plate. "This is a tough exam. Are you getting nervous, Malc? I didn't know you got nervous."

"Illogical. I am a Mobile Aid to Law and Crime," Malc responded. "Without a nervous system, I cannot get nervous."

"Confirm the inscription on the back of the watch, please."

"Capital C, dot, capital S, dot. Love, comma, capital F, dot, capital E, dot."

"Mmm." Luke walked slowly around the specimen again. The school instructors had a stock of skeletons somewhere. They were dragged out one at a time for practice and examinations. Clearly, this one was supposed to mimic a murder victim who had lain naked and undisturbed for five years or so. "No blood, no hair, no DNA, not even tendons or ligaments left, no traces of clothing. No flesh, so no evidence of flesh wounds. A completely clean male skeleton with no possessions except a pairing ring and a watch. The only sign of violence is a knife wound that probably missed the heart, too easy for an advanced exam. No, I've got to be a bit more imaginative. Give me an ultraviolet scan."

Under Malc, the white bones began to glow.

"Ever thought of a career as a spotlight in a nightclub?" Luke asked with a wicked smile. As soon as Malc bathed the skull in crisp blue light, Luke spotted a faint glimmer from deep inside an eye socket. He cried, "Stop. Home in on the right eye area, will you? What's that?"

"A thin slice of Fluoroperm 60, circular in shape."

"Ah. An old contact lens, you mean. Now we're flying. What type is it?"

"It was made to correct severe shortsightedness," Malc answered.

"Can you measure the prescription?"

"Yes."

Luke smiled and shook his head. "Go on, then."

"To measure it accurately, the lens would have to be rehydrated in saline solution. . ."

Luke interrupted. "How long does this exam last? Just compare your best estimate with the optician's database and tell me which men match that prescription."

"Within experimental error, there are three hundred and fifty-seven matches. In alphabetical order, they are. . ."

"Stop," Luke cried. "Perhaps I'm not quite flying yet. Filter out all those who are the wrong height. How many left?"

"Eighty-seven."

"Taxiing onto the runway," Luke muttered to himself. "Our man's got perfect teeth. Take out everyone who's known to have fillings."

"Thirty-four remaining."

"How many with the initials CS?"

"Three."

"How many have a partner with initials FE?"

"Two," Malc replied.

"Two? Not one? Are you sure?"

If a machine could wear a look of indignation, Malc would have worn it.

Luke held up both hands. "Yeah. All right. You're sure. You would have told me if there'd been any doubt."

Luke hesitated, wondering where he'd find the inspiration to make the final choice. He glanced back at the strong bones of the left leg and then smiled to himself. "Does your database have any personal details on these two men?"

"Confirmed, but it is not complete."

"Okay. Tell me if one of them was. . . let me guess. . . a high-jumper."

"Correct," Malc replied.

"Lift off! That's him. So, who's our short-sighted friend?"

"Colin Stanley."

Luke laughed. "Do I detect a hint of relief in your synthesized voice?"

"Illogical. Without a nervous system, I cannot experience emotions."

Luke retorted, "Oh yeah? You almost sighed."

"I must remind you that you still have to establish the cause of death – since you do not wish to consider stabbing."

"Okay, Malc. Time for you to do a bit more work – a chemical analysis on the contact lens. You see, the examiners put it there and they think, because it's given me the victim's identity, I'm going to look somewhere else for the cause of death. But I don't think I've squeezed all the juice out of it yet."

Malc recorded the infrared and ultraviolet signatures

of the contact lens and then reported, "It has not got any juice. . ."

Luke interrupted. "Never mind. I just want to know if any dodgy chemicals got out of our Colin's body in his tears. If he was poisoned, maybe there'll be a trace in his contact lens."

"When the lens dried out, it trapped within it a small amount of cyanide. It has a very distinctive infrared spectrum."

"Bob's your uncle! Evidence for soft tissue damage without even having any soft tissue."

"Being non-human, I do not have an uncle of any name."

"As a team player, Malc, you're pretty cool but, on a scale of nought to ten, you score minus one for sense of humour."

"On a scale of nought to ten, there is no minus one," Malc retorted. "For the purposes of completing the examination, you are required to state your findings."

"Boring." Knowing that Malc would be relaying his performance to The Authorities, Luke took a deep breath and said, "Colin Stanley suffered a non-lethal stab wound with a narrow blade but was probably killed by cyanide poisoning."

At once, a woman's voice, speaking through Malc, boomed into the classroom. "Congratulations. An impressive performance with which to graduate. At sixteen, you're the youngest person to pass all of the criminology tests and complete school. Your first assignment will be given to you soon." The detached voice of The Authorities paused and then added, "Just for the record, tell me why you thought the victim was a high-jumper."

Luke smiled. "The bone's much more developed in the left leg, like it did a lot more work than the right, and there's evidence of impact damage – especially in the knee – so it took quite a hammering as well. I thought it might be a high-jumper's take-off leg. That's all. Just a lucky guess."

"More astute than lucky, Forensic Investigator Harding. You've got a very sharp eye. Keep your mischievous streak in check and you'll do well."

Chapter Two

Sunset was about an hour away. At the far end of the playing field, Crispy shuffled nervously and looked at his watch. It was nearly time. His heart raced a little faster. What he was doing was against the law but he could not help himself. It felt right even if The Authorities had declared it to be wrong.

He gasped, thinking for an instant that he'd caught sight of movement at the left-hand side of the pavilion, but there didn't seem to be anybody there. The only motion was at the edge of the grounds where there was a line of ten monsters. The wind turbines droned as their huge blades turned slowly, providing the school's electricity.

The firing range was deserted. At the end of the last lesson, the students would have packed up all of the equipment. An instructor would have put it away in the pavilion and the caretaker would have checked that the area had been cleared. Crispy was sure that he was alone.

But he wasn't. By the time that Crispy noticed something hurtling towards him, it was too late. He hardly recognized the arrow before it thudded heavily into his chest. He staggered back yet kept on his feet for a moment. In that split second after the impact, he felt nothing but shock. Strangely, there was no pain. Perhaps he was beyond pain. He was standing alone on the firing range with a stick jutting out ridiculously from his chest. And he was dying.

He lifted his right hand, about to clutch the shaft, but could not manage it. His arm flopped back to his side and his eyes rolled upwards. He leaned further and further back until his body fell lifelessly to the ground.

Jade pointed enthusiastically to a panel that occupied a large part of the left-hand wall. "All that," she announced, "is a flat loudspeaker. Same on the other side." She jerked her thumb towards an identical flat panel on the right of the studio. "It's the latest wall-of-sound technology and it's going to flood this space with noise – totally. You won't be able to think. You'll just hear and feel music. Ready?" she asked with a huge grin.

Really, Luke had come to talk about exam results but Jade never got excited or depressed by passing or failing. Besides, he knew that she wouldn't want to react to his results – or talk about her own – in Malc's presence. "Where's all the furniture?" he asked.

"I've taken it out so it doesn't interfere with the sound."

"What about us? Won't we interfere with it?"

Jade laughed. "Yes, but there's no way round that, is there? We'd get a purer sound without us but we wouldn't be here to appreciate it. Now, are you ready?"

"What makes me think this is going to be an ordeal?" Seeing Jade's expression of rebuke, Luke nodded. "Ready."

Starting gently, Jade stroked her fingers across the guitar strings, forming a solitary chord.

The air around Luke's entire body throbbed with sound. "Wow."

Jade said, "It's like taking a bath but using music instead of hot water. Complete immersion."

"Gorgeous."

"Not just gorgeous. It can be vicious. Listen." She put down the guitar and pressed her remote control.

Jade's computer began her programme of drums, bass and sampled sound, adding layer after layer. Every sound was distinct and it bombarded the whole of their bodies. As the music built up, Luke seemed to hear it not just through his ears but through his skin. He was reminded of X-rays that pass straight through skin and flesh to hit bone. The experience was much more intimate than being in a noisy night-club. In the school's sound studio, Luke could have been surrounded by all of the original musicians, each playing for him alone. Soon, the added samples reached a crescendo. When Luke looked at Jade she had her eyes closed, still lapping it up when it was getting too painful for him. He touched her elbow but didn't attempt to talk. He grimaced and put his hands over his ears.

Jade touched the remote control and the music faded. "Good, eh? Enough to wake the dead."

"Yeah, but not the skeleton I've just been working on."

Malc chipped in, "It could not awaken any dead. . . "

Luke sighed, walked to the door and opened it. "Wait outside, will you, Malc?" He watched his mobile computer float past and then shut the door again. Turning back to Jade, he said, "I bet you flew through your final exam."

"I'm a fully qualified musician and audio technologist. You?"

"If anyone pinches your musical ideas, let me know. FI Harding will be after them in a flash."

Jade beamed. "Well done. I knew you'd stroll through."

In the centre of the room, they came together in a celebratory hug.

Jade was more than a musician. She lived, breathed and oozed music. It had never occurred to her that she might do anything else. In Year 8, when Luke had opted to devote his final three years to criminology, Jade had chosen music. Actually, there hadn't been a real choice for her. She had done so little work on any other subject that she had only one way forward.

Jade was much shorter than Luke and she had unruly

hair that changed colour at regular intervals. This week she was streaky blonde but Luke preferred it when she was redheaded. Her skin was a slightly paler shade of the normal brown colouring and she was pleasantly plump. She was also kind and dedicated. To Luke, Jade was definitely more than a musician. She was the only girl he had ever fancied.

Even while they celebrated together, Luke was saddened. Graduation – the end of school – meant that he wouldn't automatically see Jade every day. Their different professions would soon separate them because they would both leave Birmingham. Most crime was committed in the South of England while all of the best cultural centres for music were north of the capital. Worse still, it pained Luke enormously to know that, when The Time for pairing came, they would not be classed as suitable for each other. He dreaded The Time that threatened to part them for ever and he believed that Jade felt the same way.

Jade disengaged from him. "I still don't know how you can mess around with dead bodies and crime scenes. Yuck. Where's the warmth in that? At least music's alive."

Reluctantly, Luke let go of her arm. "So's a body and a crime scene," he replied. "Sort of, anyway. They're buzzing with clues. What's better, not everyone can see them. I've got a knack for uncovering other people's secrets and finding out exactly what happened."

"I remember that archery competition you won a year back. You beat everyone and shredded the centre of the target. You had a great eye for any sort of shooting. You should have been in sport."

Luke knew what she was getting at, but he couldn't bring himself to say anything about their coming separation. "Yeah, but there's no real future in being able to shoot straight, is there? It's fancy, but pretty useless. It's better to be the one who mops up after somebody else has done the shooting."

Jade groaned and refused to drop the subject. "But if you were a sportsman, you'd be able to live in the North. With me." She paused before adding, "Even better, I wish you'd gone into the arts. I don't need to tell you why. Now, you're going to have to go. . . you know."

The South had a terrible reputation, of course. Everyone said the people were rough and the buildings were all slums but Luke didn't really believe in those generalizations. Down south, he wouldn't have the comforts that he enjoyed in Birmingham but it couldn't be that bleak. Just because London and Bristol were decaying ports and Cambridge was full of prisons, it wasn't fair to tar the whole of the South with the same brush. He knew it wouldn't have the sophistication and beauty of Manchester, Leeds or the Peaks and it

wouldn't have the amenities of Birmingham or Sheffield but he refused to believe that the South was a dump occupied solely by savages. The real problem – the tragedy – was that it wouldn't be occupied by Jade. He said, "I'm not one of those who says you shouldn't venture south of Birmingham."

"I know," Jade muttered sadly. "Even so. . . " She shook her head.

"We're not going to solve this here and now, are we?"

"I suppose not." Jade hesitated for a few seconds and then tried to perk up. "Hey. Let me show you my new project. It's the opposite of wall-of-sound. You could call it personal music. You know, if you get a bunch of people in a dark room, it's easy to light up just one of them with a torch and leave the rest in the dark. Well, I can do the same with sound."

"You what?"

"Until now, sounds from a speaker have always spread out so everyone around can hear, but I can fire a thin beam of sound at someone like a spotlight. If you step outside the beam, you can't hear a thing. Genius. I'm pumping people their own private music. In a room or a plane or whatever, I can deliver different sounds to different people. I'll just set it up so you can. . . "

The door burst open under Malc's electronic control and the mobile computer zoomed in. Talking to Luke, Malc announced, "Your first assignment has been transmitted to me."

"What? Already?" Luke had imagined that he'd get at least a few days' break after graduating.

"Confirmed," Malc replied. "The assignment takes immediate effect."

Luke glanced at Jade and then asked, "Where is it?"

"In school."

"Here?" Luke and Jade both exclaimed at the same time.

"You are required on the sports ground without delay."

"This isn't another exercise, is it?"

"Negative," Malc answered.

"What's happened?"

"I have been informed that Instructor Thacket has found a human body."

When Luke turned towards Jade, she nodded to indicate that she understood that he had to dash. Luke took off down the corridor with Malc hovering at his shoulder.

Chapter Three

It seemed to Luke a ridiculous, medieval way to die. The boy was lying at the far end of the firing range, an arrow protruding almost vertically from his chest. He looked like a forgotten extra left behind after a film crew had finished recreating some historic battle at the location.

In his course, Luke had been told how he would react when he came face-to-face with his first real murder. His instructors had not exaggerated the impulse to freeze completely or to run away. They'd mentioned the overwhelming feeling of disgust, an outbreak of nerves and a need to be sick, but not the dreadful hammering in his chest. He tried to put aside his emotional shock and concentrate on his training but it wasn't easy. This was real flesh and blood, real life and real death. It was very different from an artificial school project where no one got hurt, where there would be one clear answer, where clues were guaranteed and the worst result of a mistake was a low mark. Here, the worst result of a wrong deduction was an innocent person given the death penalty and the murderer getting away with it.

This time, there was no need for smart technology and smart thinking to establish the victim's identity.

Luke knew the boy. He was – or had been – a quiet Year-10 student who was said to be following in Luke's footsteps. There were even rumours that Crispin Addley, or Crispy as he was usually known, was performing better than Luke had done a year ago. Luke took no interest in that type of competition but he had heard that Crispy regarded him as a rival.

It was a typical October day. Warm sunshine took the edge off the cool wind. Even so, Luke shuddered. He thought of that collection of 206 bones in his final exam. When nothing was left of Crispy but a skeleton, there would probably be nicks in two of his ribs where the sharp metallic arrowhead scraped its way between his bones and into his vulnerable heart.

Luke looked up at Malc and announced, "For the record, the victim is Crispin Addley, killed apparently by a single arrow to the heart." Luke touched Crispy's arms, neck and face lightly with the back of his hand. "He's warm and limp. His earlobes are nearly blue." Putting on medical gloves, Luke squeezed the ear between forefinger and thumb and watched it go pale as the pooled blood moved away through capillaries that had not yet been shut down by death. "The colour's not fixed yet. He's been dead less than four hours. Any rigor mortis, Malc?"

"I detect the first signs of stiffening in the face. At this temperature, it suggests death one to three hours ago."

"Let's get more accurate, if we can," Luke said. "Don't lecture me about how difficult it is. I know. Just take his temperature, estimate his weight and calculate the time of death."

"In this posture, with that amount of clothing, under the prevailing weather conditions, assuming normal body temperature when shot, the time of death is ninety minutes ago, plus or minus thirty minutes."

"Measure potassium released into the vitreous humour of his eye and try another calculation."

"Same result. Time since death is one to two hours."

"Okay. Log that time, Malc. Roughly between four and five o'clock." Luke paused. There were so many things to check out. School exercises were fairly clean and contained, but an actual crime scene was far messier, with so many factors to consider. Luke was scared in case he missed something. "Is there anything on the arrow shaft?"

"Confirmed."

"What?"

"Two partial fingerprints," Malc reported. "Both are weak."

"Are they in your databank?"

"Processing." Four seconds later, Malc came up with an answer. "Negative."

"Pity. I bet you'd have had them if this was a school test."

"Irrelevant."

"Yeah, I know." Luke let out a long breath. "There's quite a lot of blood on him but none round about, and the grass hasn't been disturbed or flattened. He was murdered on the spot, not somewhere else and dragged here. And no one's interfered with his body. So, how about this? You should be able to work out where the arrow came from using the depth of the wound, the angle of entry and how he fell. And don't say yes or no. Just do it and go to the most likely spot."

Malc completed the calculation quickly and flew to the left-hand side of the pavilion.

When the mobile returned, Luke remarked, "That's a long way away – and a difficult shot. Do we know anyone at school that good at archery?"

"Only one student in my database has the required skill."

"Don't tell me!" Luke cried. He could guess that the records showed that he himself topped the list for accurate shooting. "Scan the whole field for any objects and impressions, concentrating on the position to the left of the pavilion, will you? Video everything."

Malc said, "That will take five minutes and twenty-eight seconds."

Trying to recapture his natural manner, Luke replied, "Spoil yourself. Do a really good job and make it a round six minutes."

23

"The extra seconds will not affect the quality of the data."

Luke smiled for the first time. "Just do it and log everything for me to look at later." He knew that the cracked ground was too hard to hold footprints but he was determined to be thorough. Besides, even if the autumn rains had come and provided a soft surface that could retain impressions, the field would have been a mosaic of the soles of everyone in the school.

Turning back to the victim, Luke's smile disappeared. Weren't the dead supposed to be at peace? Weren't their faces supposed to reflect a final, inner calm? Crispy was not at rest. He looked shocked and cheated.

As a forensic investigator, Luke had many powers. He could demand fingerprints and blood samples from suspects and witnesses. He could confiscate personal effects if he believed that they would serve as evidence. He could interview anyone and his Mobile Aid to Law and Crime would record everything – or almost everything – for use in any later trial. Malc was programmed to accept all information gained by lawful methods and to reject facts that Luke obtained by untrustworthy, inappropriate or illegal means. There was one power that Investigator Harding did not have. He could not revive the dead. Right now, he would have exchanged his every achievement for that one gift. It would have been so much more useful to Crispy than the skill of investigating suspicious deaths.

The firing range was an out-of-the-way corner of the playing fields. Looking towards the main school buildings, the land rose gradually and then fell away again. The classrooms and accommodation blocks were hidden behind the mound. The firing range was always lively during sports lessons, but no one went there afterwards. Not officially anyway. It was creepy and quiet except for the constant hum of the wind turbines. Beyond Crispy, the giants would have had the perfect view of the events on the field a couple of hours ago but they remained aloof from human squabbles.

While Malc completed the environmental scan, Luke made a mental list of things to do. He needed to talk to Crispy's friends, his enemies and his instructors, especially Ms Thacket, who had discovered but not approached his body.

Luke wished that the murderer had been much closer to the victim. If there had been a struggle, the killer would have had scratches or bruises – evidence that would have lasted for days. Under the fingernails of the victim, there would have been blood and fragments of skin from the killer. Trapped between the desperate, grasping fingers, there would be shreds of the attacker's clothing or hair. In this case, Luke had been denied all of that priceless information.

Malc returned and reported that there were fifty-six artefacts within the parameters Luke had set. "None of them," Malc added, "can be linked to the crime for certain."

"Thanks. We'll go through them later. Just in case, scan his body for foreign matter or anything suspicious."

Completing the task in less than a minute, Malc said, "All matter logged. You should note four human hairs that do not belong to the victim. Black, not dyed, all roughly thirty centimetres in length."

"Okay. Do DNA profiles on the roots later and store the information. Anything on his shoes to tell me where he was before he came here?"

"Negative."

"I want to take a look in the weapons storeroom before anyone disturbs the bows."

"Are you authorizing removal of the body?" asked Malc.

"Yes. Have it taken away to pathology. I can't do any more without protective clothing or I'll contaminate the body. I want all his clothes, the contents of his pockets, the arrow and any other bits and pieces in my quarters later today. And there's something else." He swallowed uncomfortably. "Crispy always took lunch in the school canteen. I saw him. So, we know exactly what he ate and when. Get the pathologist to look at the extent of its digestion. It's not reliable, I know, but it might help us pin down when he was shot."

"Transmitting message to pathology technicians now." Then Malc followed Luke obediently back across the playing field towards the room in the pavilion where the firearms and other weapons were stored.

Chapter Four

The bunker had a high-security door and access was restricted. Now that Luke had graduated in criminology, though, he had a right of entry but his updated identity card had not yet been delivered. He pointed to the combination lock and said, "Open it, Malc."

The airborne robot beamed the correct code into the mechanism and the door clicked open. As soon as Luke walked in, the light came on automatically in the windowless bunker. The shotguns, pistols and ammunition were kept in sealed cabinets, protected by another code, but the bows were stored in open racks and the arrows were bunched in two large quivers. Without touching anything, Luke strolled along the row of bows. There were about thirty of them and there was nothing obvious to distinguish one from another.

Talking to himself, Luke asked, "Why a bow and arrow?" Answering himself, he muttered, "Because it's a silent weapon? Or because the killer's plain weird?" To Malc, he said, "Give me a list of everyone who's cleared to enter this room."

"Two sports instructors: Ms Thacket and Mr Bromley. A technician called Ella Fitch and the caretaker, Rick Glenfield. Forensic Investigator Luke Harding and all of the school management team."

Putting his gloves back on, Luke extracted two handfuls of arrows and spaced them out on a table. "Take a look at the bows, Malc. And these arrows. Have any got fingerprints that match the ones on Crispy's arrow?"

"They all have many fingerprints. Laser enhancement is necessary."

Luke closed his eyes and, to make sure, put his palms over them. "Ready."

The door shut and Malc turned off the light before flooding the racks and table with intense laser light. "Finished," Malc reported as he switched the normal light back on. "Processing."

"Everyone in school has probably handled the bows and arrows at some point," said Luke. "That's why they're plastered with prints."

After a few minutes, Malc came to a conclusion. "There are some possible matches but there are not enough points of similarity to be certain. In addition, they are obscured by overlapping patterns."

"How about a bit more enhancement with your amazing fluorescent dye?"

"The analysis is too complex to yield valid results."

"Pity. Forget prints, then."

"I do not delete anything. The fingerprint evidence is stored in my archive but it does not pass the strict conditions to be entered into case notes. However, my programming requires me to instruct you to take a set of fingerprints from an obvious suspect."

Luke held up his hands in a kind of surrender. "Yeah, I know. You want mine. I'm on the hit list because I've got the necessary shooting skills and access to this storeroom."

"School records indicate that Crispin Addley might have eclipsed your achievements. I suggest you consider that as a possible motive."

Luke smiled wryly. "Thanks for telling me my motives. I thought I was the one who did the thinking. But I never felt threatened by him."

The invisible beam swept over both of Luke's hands in an instant. Malc said, "I am programmed to assume that suspects may not tell the truth."

"Don't you feel embarrassed about this?" Luke asked.

"I do not have the capacity for embarrassment. My first allegiance is to the law. My second is to you."

"Where was I one or two hours ago, Malc? Weren't you with me? You always are. You're my alibi."

"Not quite. Seventy minutes ago, there was a period of fourteen minutes and thirty-eight seconds when. . ."

"Yeah, all right. A boy needs his privacy sometimes, you know."

"Your fingerprints are identical to those on the arrow."

"What?" Luke exclaimed.

"Your fingerprints are identical. . ."

"Yes, I heard. This is crazy! Absolutely bizarre. Am I the prime suspect in my first murder case?"

"Confirmed."

"Next, you'll be saying I've got to arrest myself!"

"That is premature. At this stage, you are far from proving your guilt."

Luke shook his head in exasperation. "Get your electronic pulses round this, Malc. Did I get you to open the weapons bunker door an hour or so ago?"

"Negative, but, as an investigator, you have the authority to access the code through other terminals, like the school computer."

"Interrogate the computer. Have I requested the code?"

"Negative. However, you have an excellent record in information technology. It is possible that you have deleted all trace of your access. There was an incident of hacking in Year 7. . . "

"Oh, come on. There's a world of difference between this and fixing Jade's science scores so she passed something other than music. This is murder!"

"Your abilities are a matter of record," Malc replied. "I cannot delete that."

Luke's mobile was invaluable, an amazing machine and almost a friend, but Malc was also as unforgiving as a brick wall. As a piece of fancy technology rather than flesh and blood, Malc believed only in facts and logic.

Trust was not a part of the computer's programming.

"What do you want me to say?" Luke snapped. "It's a fair cop, Guv?"

"Is that a confession?"

Luke shook his head impatiently, reminding himself that the result of a mistake could be an innocent person given the death penalty. He had no intention of being that person. "Come on. I have to talk to some people. I want to turn the tables on all those instructors who used to fire lots of horrible questions at me."

Chapter Five

Instructor Thacket was too lean to be considered attractive but her skin was typically brown and beautiful. Over the years, endless running had shaped her body and her muscles bulged like a man's. She ran kilometres before breakfast, she ran between lessons, she ran for the county. She pounded every path through and around the school. She taught general sport but she specialized in running. She also specialized in being vindictive. In her lessons, she was always friendly with anyone who was keen on sport but unduly harsh with students who preferred to concentrate on academic work. For them, she turned every sports lesson into physical punishment.

Now, Luke relished an opportunity to give her a hard time. Besides, his training told him to be wary of people who claim they've stumbled across a suspicious death. Some criminals tried to deflect suspicion from themselves by reporting their own crimes. Luke asked, "How did you come across Crispin?"

Ms Thacket did not waste words. "I was on a run."

"Did you recognize him?"

"Yes."

"But you didn't go up close?"

"No," she replied abruptly.

"Why not? Didn't you think he might need help?"

"It was pretty obvious he was dead and I'm not supposed to disturb a crime scene, am I?" Her stern expression seemed to be fixed on her face. It would break into a smile only when she was back among her favourite students.

Luke knew that she loved the athletic pupils, disliked the weak, and reserved special venom for students like him. Luke was brilliant at sport but he'd chosen to snub it. He went on, "Did you see anyone else in the area?"

"No one."

"This was five-thirty?"

Ms Thacket answered, "Thereabouts."

"Crispin was a clever student, wasn't he?"

"Yes."

"But hopeless at sport?"

"Totally."

That meant Instructor Thacket didn't like him. She'd probably tortured him with exercise. "Did you happen to go in to the weapons storeroom today?"

"No."

"You teach archery, don't you?"

Ms Thacket looked at him severely but didn't reply.

Nodding towards Malc, Luke said, "I'm recording this interview. I need a clear answer."

Reluctantly, she muttered, "You know I do."

"Has anyone asked for extra coaching recently?"

"Not that I know about."

Luke asked, "Is my score still the school record?"

"Yes." Her sharp tone made it clear that she wished someone else held the top slot.

"Have you got anything to do with storing the bows and arrows?"

"Of course. After each lesson."

"Are any bows missing?" Luke enquired.

"Children will be children."

"What do you mean?"

The instructor's hair was the same colour as Luke's — jet-black — but it was much shorter. Running her hand through it, she said, "There's always one or two missing. They turn up sooner or later — after some harmless prank."

"Mmm. Not all pranks are harmless, it seems."

Ms Thacket merely stared angrily at him.

He walked away from her for a few paces, but then stopped. Turning back, he shrugged his shoulders and said, "It doesn't really matter. Just a thought. Do you staff ever have archery competitions?"

"Too busy."

Smiling, Luke added, "I bet none of them would beat you."

"I wouldn't say that," she replied, not falling for Luke's flattery.

"What *would* you say?"

"I told you. We never have time for competitions."

As soon as Luke left Instructor Thacket's quarters, he said to Malc, "Does your database on archery include the school staff?"

"Negative."

"So, any of them could be a better shot than me."

"That is a possibility."

"On top of that," Luke added, "anyone could've had intensive training since their marks were last entered into the records."

"That is speculation," Malc replied. He paused and then added, "I have to prompt you to act on significant new information from Instructor Thacket."

"That bows go missing," said Luke.

"As you already have a prime suspect. . . "

Luke stopped walking and interrupted. "You want me to search my own rooms in case I'm hiding an archery bow!"

"Correct. That is the logical course of action."

"It might be logical to you but it's stupid. Don't insult my intelligence, Malc. If I'd killed Crispy, I wouldn't hide the bow in the place you know inside out. Sometimes, I wish you did think and not just deduce the logical course of action."

"I log your objection."

"Later tonight, I'm going to see Jade. If you want to waste your time and batteries, you can turn my place upside down while I'm out."

"That is an unnecessary, unhelpful and impossible method of conducting a search."

The whole school seemed downcast. The news of Crispin Addley's fate had silenced even the noisy areas like games rooms. All of the evening's activities had been cancelled and The Authorities had called for quiet contemplation.

Crispy's stunned classmates couldn't think of a single reason why anyone would want to kill Crispy. He didn't have a single enemy. Some of them even doubted that he could have been the intended victim. His best mate, a boy called Shane who had exactly the same skinny build and hairstyle as Crispin, was standing in the biology labs. He was dressed entirely in blue denim. A member of the after-school animal club, Shane was gazing in awe at the reptile house where a large snake was slowly devouring a whole squirrel.

"That's gross," said Luke, as the squirrel became an ugly bulge in the rattlesnake's body and its bushy tail poked out from the self-satisfied snake's mouth.

"Is it?" Shane replied. "I think it's really sleek." He seemed to be spellbound by the squirrel's death.

Luke hoped that the boy's detached mood was merely his way of mourning for his lost friend. "I know this isn't a good time. . ." he began.

37

Shane turned on him, venting his anger. "You're a pain. Do you know that? Always have been. If our marks drop a bit, the instructors throw you at us every time. 'Luke Harding's marks didn't slip. Diamond performance.' Only Crispy had a chance of living up to it. And look what's happened to him."

Luke guessed that Shane's grief made him hit out at an easy target. He doubted that Shane was really thinking about results when his friend had just been killed. Even so, Luke was dismayed to learn that his results were paraded in front of the younger students to make them work harder. Defending himself, he said, "That's not my fault. You should blame the instructors, not me." He noticed that it was only his grades that were used as a benchmark. He had probably not been held up as a model pupil because he'd been neither hardworking nor well-behaved. He knew that the school had always regarded him as a rebel. A very bright rebel. "Anyway, I need to ask you about Crispy."

Shane looked at Luke as if *he* were the sly and treacherous snake.

"When was the last time you saw him?"

"After school."

"What time would that be?"

"About four o'clock, I guess," said Shane.

"What were you doing?"

Shane shrugged. "Nothing. Hanging out."

"Where?"

"Nowhere near the field. Outside the greenhouse. We'd just come off duty there."

Luke smiled, trying to be friendly. "The greenhouse. One of my favourite places. I used to nick the pomegranates. I still would, but I'd be reported." He jerked his head towards his Mobile Aid to Law and Crime. "Where did Crispy say he was going when he left you?"

Shane turned back to the rattlesnake. Behind the glass, the last visible trace of the squirrel's tail had gone and the contented snake was settling down to begin the lengthy process of digesting the large lump. At the end of its curled body, its ribbed rattle stood upright ominously.

An attractive Year-11 biology student called Georgia Bowie walked across the room and smiled at the newly qualified investigator. Luke nodded, waited for the door to close behind her, and then repeated his question. Again, Shane did not answer. "Come on," Luke said. "It's very important. You can't get him into any trouble now."

"He didn't say."

Luke shook his head. "I'd rather you didn't answer than lie. Lies mislead. No answer means I just have to look somewhere else."

"Okay. Do that then."

"Obviously you don't want me to find out what

happened to your best mate."

Refusing to rise to the bait, Shane kept his eyes on the rattlesnake.

Before he left, Luke decided to try a guess. He wondered if Shane was being cagey because Crispy had gone to the far end of the field to meet a girl. A year ago, Luke had done exactly the same with Jade. Remembering the hairs found on Crispy's clothing, Luke said, "Was he meeting the nice-looking one with black hair, about so long?" He held his hands thirty centimetres apart and watched Shane's reaction to his bluff.

Shane's only reply was a deep blush.

Chapter Six

Back in his room, Luke sat in the pyramid of light from his desk lamp. He was going through the contents of Crispin's pockets and his clothes, one by one, finding nothing helpful. On his computer, he examined the data that Malc had collected from the fifty-six items near the crime scene. None of them leapt out at him as significant to the case, but one really surprised him. "What's this doing here?" he said, pointing at the image on the screen. Malc had photographed a small lizard on the yellowed grass. It was off-white in colour with grey bands and a soft pink on its head and legs.

"It is probably looking for spiders, flies and other insects."

"But is it supposed to be here? Is this its natural habitat?"

"Negative. It is a lizard of the family *Gekkonidae*, very common in warmer climates, and usually nocturnal."

"So, it's an escaped pet. And it's confused."

"That is the likely explanation."

Luke hesitated and then said, "Malc? Have you ever heard me say negative?"

"Negative."

"That's because it sounds stupid, like a robot. It's too

big a word for a simple idea. When you feel the urge to say 'negative', just say, 'no'. Short and to the point. Okay?"

"I have logged your request."

Luke's smile disappeared when he turned his attention to the arrow in a clear plastic sleeve. He was puzzled as to why a piece of sports equipment had been used as a murder weapon, but it wasn't just that. Something about the arrow still bothered him. He wished he could work out why he felt uneasy about it.

Luke said, "Until I identify who did it, I'll give him – or her – a codename. Demon Archer feels right to me." He paused before announcing to Malc, "Tomorrow morning, we search Crispy's quarters – just in case it tells me anything." Luke was convinced that Shane was protecting a girl so he added, "And I'll speak to Crispy's girlfriend."

Malc was perched on the edge of the desk, recharging himself. "Even if such a person exists, you do not know who she is."

"I will in the morning. If she's innocent, she'll be devastated. She won't turn up for lessons or, if she does, she'll be upset, to say the least."

"Speculation."

"Want to bet on it?"

"I do not bet. . . "

"Just put an order out to all instructors. They'll have

a good few students needing counselling, no doubt, but tell them to inform you if they've got an absent or particularly stressed girl with shoulder-length black hair. Of course, if she killed him, it won't work because she'll be doing her best to act normally. But, judging by Shane's red face, those hairs are probably hers so I'll get her through her DNA sooner or later, even if I have to take samples from every black-haired girl in the school." Luke stood up. "Right now," he announced, "I need to see Jade. You carry on recharging, then feel free to search the place as much as you like. I'd really appreciate it if you can find all my missing socks while you're at it, and match them up with the odd ones."

"That is outside my area of duty."

"Joke, Malc. See you later."

The students and staff of Birmingham School were lucky. They had good equipment and their living quarters were great. A lot of schools in the north were not as smart and those in the south were slums in comparison. Jade's rooms were almost identical to Luke's. They both had standard Year-11 apartments. The living room wall opposite her door had burst into life, transformed into a large telescreen. Jade was watching a music video on it. It looked like the opening to a parallel world, as if she could walk through the wall into video sequence.

When Luke came in, she turned the volume down and said, "Hiya." She seemed happy to see him but, in her eyes, there was anxiety.

Wearily, Luke plonked himself down in a chair.

"Rough day?" she asked.

"Exam on Tuesday morning, qualified by lunchtime, investigating a murder into Tuesday night. Yeah. Rough."

"I caught the story on telescreen. Poor Crispin Addley, shot with an arrow. Horrible. Have you got a suspect?"

Luke smiled wryly. "Good news and bad. I've got a strong suspect, according to Malc. The bad news is. . . it's me."

"You? What?"

"Don't ask. It's a long story. And I'm pretty sure I didn't do it." He sat upright and said, "I can speak to you, tell you things I couldn't tell Malc. Like, admit a real case is tough. With a classroom exercise, Malc's got the right databases and all the information to solve the case is at the scene somewhere. Guaranteed. When it's for real, you don't get everything you need. Nothing like. The picture's not complete. I know you'll only tell me I made the wrong choice of career. . ."

Jade interrupted, "Too right."

"But you still give me sympathy – of a sort. You know, it'd be a lot easier if we had spy cameras on every corner. Especially one covering the firing range."

"You've got to be joking! We're already monitored. Every time you use your identity card, it gets recorded on some computer somewhere. That's bad enough. Besides, what about you and me getting caught on camera?"

"Yeah, I know. I agree. But it doesn't make my job any easier."

Years ago, The Authorities had ruled out closed-circuit cameras because of the intrusion on people's privacy.

"Luke?"

"Yes?"

"I need to talk to you as well."

"Oh?" He could tell by her expression and her eyes that it was something serious.

"Ms Kee saw me this afternoon."

Luke groaned at the name of the Deputy Head and Chair of the Pairing Committee.

Jade hesitated, not wanting to say what she had to say.

"And?" Luke prompted. He knew – and dreaded – what was about to happen. As a musician, Jade would be paired with an artist to produce artistically-talented offspring. Sporty types were paired with each other to provide children of enviable physique. An investigator would be paired with the scientific sort. That meant he would never be with Jade; not properly and fully.

"I'm sixteen," she said. "Only four years away from

The Time. She wants me to get friendly with Vince."

"Vince?" Luke exclaimed. "Vince Wainwright, the architect?"

Jade nodded.

Luke swore under his breath and then lapsed into silence.

"We can't rock the boat, Luke. You're part of the law now. You can't break it. The Authorities would come down on you like a ton of bricks."

Irritated, Luke got up and paced the living room like a lion caged in an animal sanctuary, but still said nothing.

"They'd ruin my career in music as well," Jade added. "I couldn't stand that."

"I know." Luke swallowed and held back his emotions. Forensic Investigators didn't cry. They just got angry. "But Vince! You deserve better than him."

"I know who I deserve, Luke." She sniffed back a tear and squeezed his hand. "But Vince knows Ms Kee ever so well. He's her pet student. If he wants to be paired with me, it'll happen."

Luke shook his head defiantly.

"There's something else," Jade said quietly, struggling to put it into words. "She spoke to Georgia about you."

It made sense. Earlier in the day, Georgia Bowie had qualified in biology with the highest set of marks in Year 11. The Pairing Committee always matched people by subject, intelligence and age.

Furiously, Luke made for the door.

Jade called after him, "Don't do anything stupid, Luke."

"Come on!" Luke shouted into his own quarters. "I've got a case to solve."

At once, Malc glided into the corridor.

"How many bows did you find?" Luke snapped.

"I have not conducted a search," Malc replied.

"Why not?"

"You would not hide an archery bow where I would find it."

"Right. I'm going to talk to everyone with access to the weapons storeroom. Bromley first. It's getting late. Let's hope he's asleep."

"But if he is asleep. . ."

"I have the pleasure of waking him up."

Mr Bromley wasn't in bed but he was relaxing in front of his own telescreen. Surrounded by lit candles, the sports instructor was watching the big news item of the day: the murder of Crispin Addley.

Luke wasn't in the mood to hold back. He went straight to the heart of his inquiry with a lie. "Someone told me you were a top archer."

Bromley puffed out his chest. "Well, I don't like to boast but. . ."

Egging him on, Luke asked, "Would you fancy your

47

chances against me?"

"If you'd have stuck with sports, maybe not, but you'll be rusty by now. Yeah, I'd take you on. No problem. I'm a very good shot."

The flickering yellow flames were releasing trails of fine soot particles into the air.

"Where were you between four and five o'clock this afternoon?"

"What? You can't seriously. . . "

"I need an answer."

Taken aback, Mr Bromley spluttered, "I've got no reason to do anything to Crispin Addley. It's ridiculous."

"Where were you?"

"You're coming on far too strong for a lad who's only qualified today."

Normally, Luke never betrayed his feelings during an interview. He would ask a trivial question and a vital one in the same tone and he never reacted emotionally to an answer. Keeping somewhere between friendly and deadpan, he hoped each witness or suspect would talk naturally, without fretting about the significance of his questions or their own replies. This time, though, he was losing patience. He turned to Malc. "Have I asked any inappropriate questions or followed an illegal line of inquiry during this interview?"

"No."

"Then you'd better remind Mr Bromley of his

obligations as an instructor. . ."

Mr Bromley butted in. "All right, all right. I'm just pointing out that you could be polite about it." He looked at the time showing in the bottom right hand corner of his telescreen. "And it's getting late."

Luke used his considerable height to loom over Bromley. He repeated, "Where were you?"

"After lessons, I went straight to the gym," the instructor answered.

"Who saw you there?"

"I was on my own. But I saw Rick Glenfield, the caretaker, on my way out. That would have been around five-thirty, I suppose."

With the cloying smell of burning candle wax in his nose, Luke stormed out, followed closely by his mobile. As he strode down the corridor, he said to Malc, "Tell me everything you've got in your files about Vince Wainwright, Ms Kee and Georgia Bowie," he hesitated before adding, "and Rick Glenfield."

Chapter Seven

Rick Glenfield had once been an instructor of Information Technology but, according to his file, he'd been demoted four years ago because of serious doubts about his competence. Now he was a caretaker, his responsibilities included keeping the weapons storeroom clean and safe.

Luke found him in his own rooms, sitting in subdued greenish light, looking into a glass cage. Like Shane, Rick Glenfield seemed to have a fascination with reptiles because inside the cage was a fat snake, about two metres long, with a flattened triangular head. It was pale orange in colour with a pattern of black arrowheads running down its back. "It's a rattlesnake," he told Luke. "*Crotalus adamanteus*. The heaviest poisonous snake around. The boss. He loves rats, rabbits and squirrels like we love steaks. And he's very aggressive."

For the moment, Luke had worked out much of his own aggression on Instructor Bromley. Feeling emotionally empty now, he intended to fill the emptiness with his investigation. "The weapons storeroom. Has anything gone missing recently?"

Rick thought about it for a few moments and then said, "No."

"Any bows or arrows?"

"I don't count arrows," he answered, "but I heard where one ended up." He shook his head sadly.

"Did you know Crispin Addley?"

"No. I must have seen him around. I'd probably know him as one of the school students but that's all."

Luke asked, "What about archery bows? I bet you count those."

"A couple went astray some time ago but no more have gone. I blame students who left school and took them, like souvenirs. Sometimes, missing ones have turned up in vacated rooms. Either way, The Authorities normally blame me."

Detecting a grievance in his voice, Luke pounced. "You once taught computing. I remember from when I was in Year 6. Why are you a caretaker now?"

"There's a great big file on me. I've seen it, but never got inside it. That'll tell you."

It seemed to Luke that Glenfield resented the fact that a forensic investigator had access to school records but a caretaker did not. "Yes. I checked it out. I know what The Authorities say but I don't know your side of the story. Maybe there's a difference."

Rick was in his mid-thirties and his homely face sat inside a ring of ginger hair. Both his beard and the hair on his head were already tinged with grey. He took a deep breath. "In those days, I installed the school's software. All the teething troubles, bugs and loopholes counted against me. My classes got lower marks than others in the same year. There were some discipline problems. And a million other things were all my fault, apparently." He shrugged. "What can they expect when they always gave me the worst kids? As for the software, it leaked like a sieve but I didn't write it. I only installed it. The other things? Well, we all have hiccups now and again. Most of the time, it was just my bad luck."

"You must have been annoyed," said Luke, trying to lead him on.

"A few staff backed me, like Ms Kee. I've always been grateful but it didn't make any difference in the end. I was destined to be a caretaker, like a maggot's destined to become a fly."

Luke wondered why Glenfield had singled out the Deputy Head but he had no wish to talk about her. Getting to his feet again, he said, "One final thing. I just wondered if you saw anyone while you did the rounds after school."

"Lots. I was making sure everything was spick and span so I didn't pay any great attention to them."

"How about near the weapons store?"

Rick shook his head. "I went there first, you know, to make sure it was secure. There wasn't anyone around apart from me."

"What time was that?"

"I looked after a detention for Ms Kee for half an hour after lessons. Then I went straight to the bunker. About four-fifteen, I guess."

"Okay." With a casual shrug of the shoulders and an expressionless face, Luke could make anyone believe they were spilling trivial titbits rather than crucial evidence. "What about near the gym?"

"I don't. . . Hang on. Mr Bromley was just leaving. His hair was all wet so I guess he'd just had a shower. That'd be nearing six by my reckoning."

"Fine," Luke replied. "That's all for now."

Luke always had a pomegranate for breakfast. The world – and Malc – had to wait until the lengthy process of eating came to an end. As Luke sliced eagerly into this morning's fruit with a sharp knife, Malc commented, "Statistics show that less than one per cent of people eat pomegranates."

"Yes," Luke replied. "If we could get the percentage up, there'd be a lot less crime."

"There is no evidence for that assertion."

"That's because I just made it up. But the bad guys would have a lot less time for crime because pomegranates take so long to eat."

Luke would begin the day bleary-eyed but he'd emerge from the breakfast table like a butterfly from a chrysalis once he'd sunk his teeth into the clusters of bright red seeds and sprayed the flavour around his mouth. Of course, he also sprayed the juice all over the table, making it look like the scene of a stabbing. Even an expert eater of pomegranates like Luke made a terrible mess.

Baiting Malc, Luke said between mouthfuls, "Pomegranates make brains grow bigger, you know. People who eat them are super smart."

"That is another unproven claim. There is no known mechanism for pomegranates to increase human brain power."

"It's because the inside of a pomegranate looks like a brain."

"There is no correlation between the appearance. . ."

Smiling, Luke said, "Malc. Let me finish on my own. This one's really good. I need to concentrate."

Ms Kee hurried along the corridor towards her office, early on Wednesday morning. For the moment, thoughts of Crispin Addley had been pushed aside by a timetable clash that Ms Thacket had spotted yesterday. She would have to sort it out with the sports instructor before school began. Ms Kee was also juggling several possible pairings. Some were causing her concern but she was convinced that Vince Wainwright was right for Jade Vernon and that Luke Harding would make an ideal partner for Georgia Bowie.

She wouldn't admit it out loud but she was proud of Luke Harding. He was living proof that her kind of discipline worked. Until recently, Luke had tasted more of her discipline than any other pupil. But it had worked. He was now a highly regarded forensic investigator. Even if Crispin Addley had lived to equal or surpass Luke, she would not have felt the same satisfaction because Crispin had never stepped out of line.

Hoping that Ms Thacket would also be heading for her office, Ms Kee glanced again at her copy of the timetable and quickened her pace. She was not concentrating on where she was going because her mind was occupied and because she expected the way to be clear. The whole place had been stilled by Crispin's murder. She let out a loud cry of surprise when she turned a corner and slammed straight into someone coming in the other direction.

She didn't see the needle and she didn't feel a thing because it was coated with a local anaesthetic. When it ripped through the skin of her right forearm, it numbed her nerves as it went. It slid easily through the epidermis and dermis, past greasy sebaceous glands, hair follicles and sweat glands, into muscle. There, the poisonous liquid in the syringe spurted through the hollow needle and into her tissue. But, with the force of the collision, the needle didn't stop. It penetrated deeper, piercing the thin wall of a vein and squirting some of the deadly fluid into the column of blood heading for her heart. Like a drop of ink in a stream of water, the poison swirled and mixed as it raced along with the blood. Once it reached her heart, it would circulate quickly, each beat of her heart sending out little packages of poison to every part of her body.

After yelping in shock, Ms Kee sighed. "You gave me a fright," she said. "Still, no harm done." She picked up a piece of paper that she'd dropped. "Anyway, come into my office. I need to have words about that business yesterday." She led the way, scratching an itch on her forearm.

If Luke had made a bet with Malc about the existence of a grieving girlfriend, he would have won. Almost as soon as school began in the morning, Malc was notified of several absences and shaken students but only one had hair that matched the description. It came as a shock to Luke when Malc reported that Olivia Pang was in Year 9 but, when Luke thought about it, things fell into place.

Crispy had been in the year above her and the Pairing Committee did not permit unions between people of different ages. No wonder Shane had kept her name to himself. He'd been trying to keep her out of trouble. Luke also realized that, whenever Crispy and Olivia had got together, they would have done so in secret. It was crucial for Luke to find out from her if they'd met yesterday, shortly after four o'clock and just before Crispy died. He also needed to know where they'd met.

Yet all his training hadn't prepared him for handling a witness with a torrent of grief pouring down her cheeks. Every last shred of her attractiveness had dissolved in sorrow. She was sitting on her bed with a sodden handkerchief clasped tightly in her hands. She had probably been awake all night and her black hair was a mess.

Instantly, Luke felt for her. Deciding what to do, he left her quarters right away. In the corridor outside, he said to Malc, "You stay here. I'm going back in to talk to her on my own."

"No," Malc replied. "That is not permitted. No suspect or witness may be interviewed. . . "

"Malc. What were my law marks?"

"One hundred per cent."

"So, I don't need you to recite it to me. I know it's not permitted."

"Any information gathered without my presence is not admissible."

Luke sighed. "Yes, I know that one too. But use your logic circuits, will you? You're very proud of them."

"I am not. . . "

"Look," Luke said, butting in again. "Believe me, she's not going to say anything with you in there recording.

That's for sure. She might not say anything to me on my own either. But there's a chance. So, if you come in, we won't get anything for the case. If you stay out, we still won't get anything for the case but I might just learn something useful. Which is better?"

"I cannot sanction an unlawful action."

"Tough. Stay out here and report me. Give The Authorities something else to put in my bad file. It must be as fat as Rick Glenfield's." He went back into Olivia's apartment and slammed the door shut.

Chapter Eight

Luke grabbed a chair and sat down opposite Olivia Pang. "I'm sorry," he said softly.

She did not respond.

"I want to tell you something," Luke continued. "Unofficially."

Olivia looked up, but immediately her head bowed again.

"I'm going to be paired with a biologist called Georgia Bowie. She's nice. I'd be the first to admit it. Bright and good-looking. Great smile, always laughing, great personality. Well-rounded figure. I should be delighted. I should consider myself lucky. If I hadn't met Jade first. . . but I did. You know Jade Vernon, do you? Musician in my year." He stressed the word musician.

Now, Olivia was looking at him, listening.

Even though it was painful to look into her tortured face, Luke held her gaze. "Yes. I fell for a musician. In a big way. You know what that means. She's someone an investigator can never be paired with. Right age, wrong type. You see, I know what it's like trying to come to terms with the rules for pairing – and failing. So, I understand a part of what you're going through. I can't imagine what it'd be like to lose Jade."

Olivia wiped her nose and cheeks with the handkerchief. "Crispy was determined to do as well as you. Better, if he could."

Luke smiled faintly. "I wish he'd had the chance."

Desperate to salvage something, she said, "I'm sure we'd have been paired if we'd been the same age."

Luke nodded and leaned forward. "I have to ask you something very important. The two of you would've planned your meetings carefully. What was your plan for yesterday afternoon?"

Olivia looked surprised. "We didn't have one."

"What? You didn't have a date after school?"

"No. Too much work."

Recovering from the unexpected answer, Luke asked, "Who'd want him out of the way, Olivia? There must be someone."

Olivia shook her head. "No."

"No one jealous or anything? Perhaps someone put out by your relationship with him?"

Her shoulders shaking, Olivia had retreated into misery again.

"If you think of anything, when you've had a bit of time, let me know. All right?"

She nodded without looking up.

"You can always come and talk to me. I can arrange for us to be private." He didn't get a reaction so he added, "You ought to know Shane didn't tell me who you were. He did his best to keep you under wraps." As he got up from the chair, Luke put a hand on her heaving shoulder. "Never be ashamed, Olivia. It's the rules that are wrong, not you and Crispy." Then he left.

Luke held up the hair that he'd lifted from Olivia's shoulder. "Scan it, Malc. Is it the same as the hairs on Crispy's clothes?"

"I can perform the DNA analysis but the result is inadmissible."

"Just tell me."

"Processing."

"Give me the result on the way to Shane's class."

Before Luke dragged Shane out of a lesson for a brief interview, Malc said, "The hair is identical with all four on Crispin Addley's clothing."

Occupying an empty common room near to Shane's class, Luke said to him, "I've found out who Crispy's girlfriend was and I think I can keep her out of the case. You know that'd be best for her at her age. But, to get me to cooperate, you'll have to make a deal with me."

Shane was frowning. "What's that?"

"You don't have to name her. You just have to answer a couple of questions."

Suspiciously, Shane replied, "Go on."

"Did Crispy definitely say he was going to meet her when he left the greenhouse yesterday?"

"Yes."

"How did he know?"

"He said he'd had a telescreen message from her."

Luke nodded. "Okay. That's all I need from you for now. As I said, I'll do my best to keep her out of it. You can go back into your class."

Without losing a moment, Luke dashed towards Crispy's quarters.

Inside the apartment, he said, "Link yourself to his telescreen, Malc, and access any messages from yesterday." With the nail of his forefinger, he flicked a pomegranate seed out from between two of his teeth.

"There is one message," Malc announced.

"What is it?" asked Luke excitedly.

"Meet me on the firing range. 4.30. Love, Olivia."

Luke raised a fist. "Yes! Now we're flying. Where did it come from?"

After five seconds, Malc said, "Untraceable."

Luke cursed as he came suddenly back down to earth. "Well, I'll tell you one thing. It didn't come from Olivia Pang."

"Speculation."

"Why would she hide its origin when she's signed it? No. It came from someone who lured Crispy out to the far corner of the field at an exact time. Olivia's hairs on his clothes could have been there for ages. They don't prove he met her yesterday. He thought he was going to meet her but all he got was an arrow." Dejectedly, Luke added, "No wonder he looked shocked and cheated." Trying to cheer himself up, Luke turned to Malc and said, "Have your logic circuits deduced anything about Demon Archer?"

"Yes."

"What?"

"He or she has sufficient computing skills to conceal the source of a telescreen message. Demon Archer is also aware of the relationship between Crispin Addley and Olivia Pang."

"Ah, those electrons are really singing. Now, ask yourself, did I know about Crispy and Olivia yesterday?"

"You did not exhibit any knowledge of it," Malc answered.

"Put that into your notes on the prime suspect."

"Entered. However, you were unusually confident of identifying her today."

Luke put his head in his hands. When he looked up, he said, "I didn't know her, Malc. Don't confuse confidence and guilt. They're quite different."

The search of Crispy's rooms did not reveal anything noteworthy. Frustrating Luke, there was nothing that pointed to a motive for murder. For the first time, he began to wonder if there was a motive. Motiveless killings were very uncommon but they did occur. Luke had been taught that they happened when someone wanted to show their power through a random killing, when the culprit was mad, or when the person murdered was not the intended victim. Luke had also been taught that cases of motiveless killings were exceptionally difficult to solve.

Malc interrupted Luke's thoughts. "The pathologist has examined the extent of digestion of Crispin Addley's last meal. Death is estimated to have taken place three and a half to four and a half hours after lunch."

"That fits," Luke replied. "It's all pointing to the four-thirty rendezvous on the field. We know when and how. If I knew why, it'd lead me to who."

Malc's neutral tone barely changed but Luke detected an added urgency when the mobile announced, "I have received another message."

"Oh?"

"You are required in Ms Kee's quarters."

It was like being back in Year 7. All the naughty pupils – Luke among them – got sent to Ms Kee. "Why?"

"At the start of school this morning, she reported feeling ill in her office. She complained of dizziness, numbness, and extreme pain in the arm. She returned to her apartment and has since died."

"She's what?" Luke exclaimed, staring at his mobile.

"She has died."

Stunned, Luke said, "Can't you register any shock at all?"

Dispassionately, Malc replied, "No. But I can inform you that the circumstances of her death are suspicious."

Chapter Nine

Luke would never have described Ms Kee as a favourite instructor. Quite the opposite. He could never force himself to like the person in charge of the Pairing Committee. But, as he examined her body with a pained grimace on his face, it struck him that no one deserved such a death. Her face and pillow were soiled with blood-spattered vomit, her clothes were drenched with her own sweat and her eyes were bloodshot. Her right arm was swollen horribly. The brown skin was stretched to its limit. A part of her forearm was about three times its normal size, blown up as big as a basketball. The skin over the enormous blister was thin and shiny like a balloon on the point of bursting. Around it, the tissue was black, totally dead. Luke gulped. Something had attacked her flesh from the inside.

"I saw this sort of thing in the Forensic Medicine module. It's the effect of an allergic reaction, isn't it, Malc?"

Unaffected by sentiment, Malc answered coolly, "Not confirmed, but likely. The sickness, fever, violent inflammation and tissue death are consistent with it. There is also evidence of muscle spasms typical of an allergic reaction."

"So, what brought it on? It's. . . grotesque. Is it

natural, an accident or some weird sort of poisoning?"

"Insufficient data."

"Yeah, I know. I'm just thinking aloud, I suppose." Luke turned away and took a deep breath. To Malc, he said, "I wish your programming allowed you to feel sick. Then you'd know how bad I'm feeling right now. Anyway, scan the swelling, microscopic scale."

Malc moved in and hovered over the bulge in the arm that reminded Luke of a snake that had swallowed an outsize rodent. "There is a single ragged puncture wound."

Luke frowned. "What do you mean by ragged?"

"It is not the neat round wound left by an injection performed by a skilled medic."

"You mean it was a rough jab."

"Correct."

"Well, I guess that rules out natural causes."

"Confirmed."

Luke sighed. "Some sort of poison was jabbed into her arm. Accident or assassination. But why get me involved? Even if it's murder, what's it got to do with the Crispy case? Different weapons, different gender, different age, different status. How many differences do you want? No, don't answer that. The only thing that connects it to Demon Archer is time and place. The school never had a murder till yesterday. Now we might have two in two days."

"That is not the only connection. The prime suspect for Crispin Addley's murder also has a motive for eliminating Ms Kee."

"What?"

"You are known to be dissatisfied with the Pairing Committee. Ms Kee is in charge of that committee. In addition, you requested information on her thirteen hours and seventeen minutes ago. I discovered in her files that she was proposing Georgia Bowie as your partner. She also anticipated the pairing of Jade Vernon and Vince Wainwright."

Luke put up his hands. "Stop! You're getting way ahead. It's one of your favourite words – speculation – until I work out if there's even been a crime. Besides, I've got an alibi. I was with you."

"For a total of forty-one minutes this morning, you were not under my supervision."

"First I was taking a shower, then I was tucking into breakfast, then I was with Crispy's girlfriend. You know that."

"You insisted upon my absence from that interview, despite my instruction."

"Okay. It looks bad but. . . You don't know the meaning of discretion, do you?"

"Noun. The capability of maintaining a prudent silence."

"Yes," Luke interrupted. "You can look it up in your

dictionary but that's about it. All these findings that make me look guilty, you're transmitting them to The Authorities' central computer, aren't you?"

"Confirmed," Malc answered. "I am programmed to do so."

"Great!"

Malc replied, "It does not seem great for you."

Luke shook his head. "It's called irony. Look it up." He didn't blame Malc, of course. Malc was a machine designed to follow set procedures. In the same way, no one could blame Luke for growing too tall. Luke was at the mercy of his genes and Malc had his programming.

So close to the body, Luke felt as if he needed another shower. Sadly, not even the hottest power-shower could wash away the awful image that had already lodged in his mind. The person on the bed was clearly Ms Kee but in a way it wasn't. It wasn't really a person at all. Not any more. The Deputy Head had gone and left behind a foul carcass for Luke to read. Steeling himself, he turned back to her wasted body.

In this new case, he would not be short of possible motives. Usually, the pairing process went smoothly, but there could be couples who were dissatisfied with Ms Kee's impact on their lives. There would also be several badly behaved students who might want to get their own back on the Deputy Head for the harsh punishments that she had dished out regularly. Of course, Malc would have already put Luke on a list of disobedient pupils who might be hungry for revenge. "Take a blood sample for analysis, please," said Luke.

"Where from?"

Luke arched his eyebrow. "There's plenty to chose from. Does it matter? Take it from around the blister if you can, without breaking the skin. If not, use the stuff caked around her mouth. Run tests for poisons."

Luke walked around the body, examining it carefully without touching, while Malc alighted gently on the exposed arm. "You said she reported being ill this morning. Who did she speak to?"

"The school secretary."

"Are you getting a blood sample?"

"Confirmed. Analysis in progress."

"I don't want to overload you," Luke said, "but there are some hairs on her lap. Scan them next." When he'd completed two circuits of the bed, Luke added, "There's not much else I can see. I want a post mortem as soon as possible."

"Preliminary blood analysis complete," Malc stated.

"Let's hear it."

"The blood cannot clot because fibrinogen levels are very low and the platelets are clumped together."

"That's why it's run into her eyes, blisters and gums."

"Correct," Malc replied. "Failure to clot has been caused by a complicated mixture of toxic proteins and

enzymes, typical of many animal venoms."

"Venom? Which animal?"

"I am performing more sophisticated tests to identify the species."

"A lizard?"

"That is one of many possibilities."

"What about the one you spotted on the field?"

"The gecko is not poisonous," Malc informed him.

"Thinking about it, biting animals wouldn't leave a single puncture mark. There'd be at least two. Could all this happen because she was allergic to a bee or wasp sting or something like that?"

"No. The venom is much more complicated than a simple sting."

"What about those hairs?"

"They are not human."

Luke smiled. "Good. Perhaps they belong to the poisonous animal."

"They are from three different individuals."

"Three?"

After a short pause, Malc announced, "They are all feline."

Luke was astounded. "She's had three cats on her lap. Is that what you're telling me?"

"Correct."

"But cats aren't poisonous and they're very scarce." Like dogs, cats were endangered animals, kept only in conservation parks. "Has she had anything to do with animal sanctuaries?"

"No contact known."

"I really need to find out which animal the venom came from, Malc. Once I know its properties, I'll be able to get moving. How quickly the poison acts will tell me when she was stung, bitten or injected. Till then, do a fine scan down her right-hand side. I'm looking for anything that's not Ms Kee's – fibres, blood, skin, fur or scales, anything out of place."

Chapter Ten

When the school secretary handed over Luke's new identity card, Malc had to witness and record the event. It was only a small piece of plastic but it gave its owner so many rights that The Authorities needed proof it had been delivered correctly. They also required Luke to say aloud and in public the simple but powerful words that every forensic investigator had to recite. "I pledge my allegiance to the law." The card identified Luke, his personal details, and his profession. At the bottom, it read 'Luke Harding, Forensic Investigator'. It was his certificate of graduation, it would grant him access to almost any building, and it gave him the full authority of an investigator. It was what he had worked towards for the last three years.

When Luke uttered his pledge and took the card in his hand, he felt a warm glow of achievement, a tingle of excitement, and a terrible weight on his shoulders. He had not just come of age. With this licence, he had joined the highest ranks. His new power thrilled and frightened him at the same time. He felt that it had arrived before he was ready for it.

As far as Ms Kee's case was concerned, the secretary wasn't much help. He stared at Luke in astonishment. "Cats?" he exclaimed. "Haven't seen one in years.

Shouldn't think Ms Kee had either. Never seen her with one."

For the record, Luke had already found out from the secretary what time Ms Kee went to her office at the start of the day and when she'd reported sick. Just before he left to continue his investigation of Crispin Addley's death, Luke asked, "Oh, did she say she'd knocked into anyone this morning, you know, in the corridor or something?"

"No."

"Did she mention any quarrels she was having?"

The secretary shook his head. "Mighty confused when she spoke to me. Said she was going back to bed."

Until Year 10, Luke had had to deal with one training exercise after another. He'd always had time to clear his mind of one assignment before starting the next. Then in Year 10, his instructors had turned up the heat. He'd have to solve three or four training cases at once. Sometimes they would be linked and sometimes not. The exercises had been designed to prepare him for handling two cases at once, for seeing subtle links, for keeping track of different threads. But back then, his mind had not been tainted with an image of a revolting, lifeless corpse stripped of all humanity.

Trying to focus his brain on archery, he went to see Ella Fitch. Ella was the technician in charge of sports equipment. When Luke and Malc walked into her windowless workshop, she was wearing a dirty overall and protective goggles as she repaired a set of starting blocks with a blowtorch. She turned off the gas supply and the fierce blue flame spluttered and then died. Lifting the goggles onto her forehead, she looked like a motorcycle racer. "Hello," she said, apparently not surprised by Luke's visit.

"I'm FI Harding."

Ella smiled. "I know who you are. To me, you'll always be Diamond who sabotaged. . . "

"Hold on. I'm who?"

"Don't you know? A lot of the staff call you Diamond."

Luke was amazed. "Do they?"

"It was one of the instructors – Mr Bromley or maybe Rick Glenfield when he was still in computing – who said, 'He's bright, and much tougher than he looks. Like a diamond.' It stuck, I guess. Even the ones you played up sometimes call you the diamond student. It's a sneaking respect, you know. Only Ms Thacket spits it out with irony. She didn't like it when you went for criminology instead of sport." Ella paused to catch her breath. "Talking of games, I was going to say, I'll always remember you for last sports day when you went in for a bit of sabotage. You know what I'm talking about."

Luke nodded. He wasn't likely to forget. He'd taken Ed Hoffman's javelin, hollowed out a section near the tip, filled it with lead and then covered it up. As a result, Ms Thacket's favourite student – and favourite for the competition – lost in grand style, his javelin too heavy and unbalanced.

Ella was giggling to herself. "I kept the javelin as a memento. Brilliant job. Nasty Hoffman strutted around, looking superior as he always does, ran up, and made a complete fool of himself in front of everyone. Really fruity. It couldn't have happened to a more deserving case."

"Yeah, but I overdid it. He complained and I got caught."

"Why did you do it? Was he bullying you like he bullies everyone else?"

"No, but I'd just seen him have a go at Travis Myers. Do you know Travis?"

"The white lad."

Very occasionally, children would be born with less skin pigment because of a faulty gene. They were normal in every way except for their colour, somewhere between light brown and white. Travis Myers was Birmingham School's only pupil with the faulty gene.

Luke said, "There's no reason to harass whites. You might as well pick on someone for having blue eyes."

Ella nodded in agreement. "No doubt it was you that

ended up in the queue of bad boys outside Ms Kee's room, not Hoffman. Once, you were a permanent feature in the line."

The blowtorch had created an uncomfortable dry warmth in the room. "Have you heard about Ms Kee?" Luke asked.

"I can't say I'm gutted, to be honest. I never did get on with her." She removed the goggles altogether as if she expected a lengthy interruption to her work. "She was too keen on discipline for my taste. Kids need a bit of freedom and mischief. That's what they're for. Still, I suppose I don't have to put up with whole classes of them. I just have to fix the stuff they break. That doesn't bother me. It keeps me in the job I love. I like the naughty ones. Not the nasty ones like Hoffman, just the naturally playful kids. Like you."

Luke sat down on a bench. "You'll know why I'm here."

She nodded. "Crispin Addley. They called him Crispy, didn't they? He was all right, I suppose. I never had to fix anything on account of him. He was one of the well behaved lads, not like some I could mention." She kept her bright eyes on Luke. "Awful what happened, though. I guess you want to know if I saw anyone on the firing range after hours yesterday. No chance. I was in here, working away on my own. You should ask Rick Glenfield. He's up there almost every day."

"Shooting?"

"No, doing his job – cleaning and so on. I've been thinking, though. It's a pity Ms Kee can't get her hands on whoever did it. Then they'd think the death penalty was the easy option."

Luke wished that every witness could be like Ella Fitch: friendly and talkative. He barely needed to ask a question to turn her on like a tap. "Have you ever seen someone wandering off with a bow?"

"Mischief's fine but that's going too far. It could be dangerous. I'd stop someone if I saw them doing that. But I can't say I have. Why? Are some bows missing?"

"Always, according to Ms Thacket." Not wanting to dwell on it, Luke changed the subject. "Do you ever see animals on the playing fields, wild or with people?"

Ella was surprised by his question but took off again. "Plenty of rabbits, squirrels, badgers and birds. Anything smaller – like mice – and I doubt I'd see them. I expect there's lots of mice because I've seen owls and bats hunting something at night. Probably mice or some such. Sometimes, sheep, cows and chickens stray over here from the farm. I bet there are others but I haven't seen them."

"How about something unusual, like dogs or cats?"

"Oh, you've heard the rumours as well," Ella replied. "Has that got anything to do with young Crispin?"

"I'm following lots of different leads at the moment,"

Luke replied. Hoping for another gush of words, he said, "So, tell me what you've heard and I'll see if it's more or less what I know."

Luckily, Malc did not interrupt to remind Luke that he hadn't heard any rumours. The mobile floated beyond Luke's shoulder, recording the interview. Luke hoped that Malc had detected a significant item, partly hidden in the far corner of the workshop, and scanned it.

Ella seemed relaxed as if she were merely enjoying a chat with Luke, rather than being under the scrutiny of Investigator Harding and his Mobile Aid to Law and Crime. "It seems fish, guinea pigs and rabbits just don't do it for a lot of animal lovers. They want the more exotic stuff. If you have a real close look at the field for long enough, you'll probably find a few that have escaped from captivity. Some of the younger kids say they've seen lizards and things, but they're very imaginative, aren't they? The kids, that is, not the lizards. Anyway, I heard there's a hard core that hankers after endangered species. Possibly even in high places. Well, it's asking for trouble, isn't it? There's an animal sanctuary down the road that keeps dogs and cats, and there are people who'd do anything to get their hands on them as pets."

"Well, that's pretty much what I've heard as well," Luke lied convincingly, "but the important point is, if cats and dogs are being smuggled, who's behind it? I haven't heard that."

"If you believe the conspiracy theories, the President, the school head and management team, quite a few pupils, you and me." With a wicked smile, Ella shrugged.

"In other words, you don't know either. It's all speculation."

"Wild rumours are always more fun than facts," she replied with a laugh.

Luke stood up again. "Well, thanks for your help."

"Anything for the brains behind my favourite stunt against my least favourite pupil." She paused before adding, "You know, I didn't shop you to Thacket over the javelin. I was more amused than anything. I was like that," she said, nodding at Malc. "I just did forensic tests on it."

"That's all right," Luke replied. "I owned up – as always."

"If you want my advice," she continued, "you should look into Ed Hoffman."

"Oh? Are you saying he clashed with Crispy?"

Ella shrugged. "No idea. He's just a nasty piece of work."

"Thanks," Luke replied politely. "Before I go, do you know if any of the school staff are crack archers?"

Ella was delighted to have the opportunity to gossip for longer. "Mr Bromley's a flashy show-off, not as good as he likes to think, but still fair. Ms Thacket doesn't shout about it, but she's been practising and she definitely knows where the target is. Me. Don't tell anyone, but I'm useless. Instructor Cadman – he must have taught you biology and the biological bits of criminology – he's another quiet one. Maybe he's the one who called you Diamond. I don't know. Anyway, he doesn't advertise it but he's a real top shot. Always out there shooting, always wearing a hat. There are plenty more, I guess."

"Rick Glenfield?"

"No idea. I've never seen him have a go, and he keeps himself to himself. His self-esteem took a bit of a battering when they made him caretaker. He doesn't put himself about much. I don't think he's the type."

Chapter Eleven

Outside, a sudden strong wind was stripping bronzed leaves from the elms dotted around the school. There was still no sign of the rains. When the storm clouds finally came, there would be huge relentless downpours.

As soon as they left the workshop, Luke said to Malc, "I hope you scanned that archery bow in the corner behind her."

"Confirmed."

"And?"

"And what?" Malc preferred unambiguous questions.

Luke spelled it out. "What, if anything, was your conclusion?"

"I could not scan all of it but the exposed areas had many identical overlapping fingerprints. They matched the fingerprints on the blowtorch."

"So, it's her personal bow," said Luke, "even though she says she's no good." He was undecided about Ella Fitch. She seemed almost too helpful, too pleasant.

"I have completed the advanced analysis of Ms Kee's blood and it is consistent with the pathologist's initial examination of the body."

Luke carried on walking towards the school exit as he listened to Malc's findings.

"I have now identified most of the toxic proteins and enzymes and compared them with a databank of animal venoms. There is a nearly perfect match with the venom of the eastern diamondback rattlesnake, *Crotalus adamanteus*. Its poison thins blood, making it so runny that it leaks out of ruptured blood vessels. This explains the blood-filled blotches underneath the skin, bruising, discoloration of skin, bleeding gums and eyes, and the severe swelling on the right forearm, all confirmed by the pathologist. Pathology also notes watery blood pooled in the extremities and lungs. Once the fluid had filled the lungs, paralysis, coma and death would follow rapidly. Probable cause of death is suffocation through internal drowning."

"Charming." Quickly, Luke put up a hand to stop Malc replying. "That's irony as well." Then he said, "But she wasn't bitten by a rattlesnake because she'd only got one puncture wound. A snake would leave two marks. Someone injected it – roughly. Possibly while barging into her like it was an accident."

"I cannot determine the quantity of venom but it was considerable. The pathologist estimates that most was injected into forearm tissue, causing local destructive effects such as gangrene. However, some penetrated a blood vessel and circulated rapidly in the blood, attacking the whole body and causing death in less than two hours."

"So, she was poisoned this morning, probably on the way to her office. The next question is obvious," Luke said to himself. "Who's got access to rattlesnake venom?"

Malc answered anyway. "The Biology Department has several of these snakes. Yesterday, you saw Shane with one of them. Also, Rick Glenfield had one as a pet in his quarters."

Reaching the school entrance, Luke put his new identity card against the security panel and at once the gates opened for him. Outside was the main freeway into Birmingham centre. Electric cabs, controlled by computer, sped past at high speed. Luke swiped his identity card through the freeway reader and said into the microphone, "The animal sanctuary."

The next cab slowed at the school gates and Luke climbed into it with Malc. As soon as Luke was seated, the cab accelerated sharply. A line of occasional wind turbines separated the freeway from the parched flatlands of the farm and fed the cab corridor with electrical power. Urged on by the wind, the massive rotating blades gleamed in the sunshine.

"If someone crashed into Ms Kee so they could jab rattlesnake venom into her arm at the same time, they'll have left traces when they came into contact. So, what did you find in that scan down her right-hand side?"

"A microscopic flake of white paint, two blue denim fibres that I cannot enter into case notes because they

are so common, one further feline hair, six fine particles of magnesite, a very faint smear of an unknown wax, and a small deposit of sawdust. The specks are too small to allow the wood to be identified."

"Magnesite?"

"Correct."

"Isn't that a white mineral?"

"Confirmed. It is magnesium carbonate, used to make heat-resistant bricks and non-slip cement for flooring in hospitals and kitchens. It has other uses in the chemical industry such as the manufacture of fertilisers."

"Mmm." Luke wasn't sure what to make of the finding so he moved on. "What about the paint? Is it new – like you'd get from leaning against wet paint – or is it an old flake?"

"It is old and brittle."

"So, she'd brushed against some peeling paintwork, or someone else did and transferred it to her when they bumped into each other," Luke reasoned. "Why can't you identify the wax?"

"The sample is too small."

"Pity."

The cab had hardly got up to its cruising speed before it began to slow down. When it pulled up outside the conservation park, Luke and Malc got out. Revelling in his new powers, Luke did not speak into the security panel and wait for a response. He drew his card over the reader to open the gate, walked straight in and made his way to the reception in the old lodge. Inside, the manager of the sanctuary agreed to take Luke to one of the cat enclosures and to answer all of his questions about smuggling. "I'm just pleased that The Authorities are taking this seriously enough to send an investigator at last." She glanced at Luke and held herself back from adding, "Even if they've picked a young and inexperienced one."

"You don't deny that animals go missing, then?"

"I run a big sanctuary here, Investigator Harding. We take lots of precautions but if someone's determined to get in, they probably will."

To the left, horses cantered across a field. On the other side was a herd of lazy zebras.

"What gets stolen?"

She shrugged. "It goes in phases. Flavour of the month is cats." She pointed ahead to the hut with a large enclosure bounded by wire netting. "Someone cuts the wire to crawl in and take one or two at a time. Cats breed quite well in captivity but whoever's doing it only goes for the most attractive pedigrees, like blue Persians, Egyptians and Siamese, and we can't afford those sorts of losses. These breeds are going to die out soon."

Beside the hut, there was a cage full of mice nestling

together in sawdust. "What are these for?" asked Luke.

"They're let loose in the cat sanctuary to provide exercise and food."

Feeling sorry for the mice on death row, Luke said, "Any idea who's behind the smuggling?"

"We almost caught a boy a week or so back. He ran off in the direction of the school so he'll be one of yours. About your age as well, I guess. But it was too dark to give you any sort of description. I got in touch with the school, though. I had words with – who was it? – a Ms Kee, I think. Something like that, anyway."

"What did she say?" asked Luke.

"She said she'd hold an inquiry and catch those responsible."

"And what happened?"

The manager smiled wryly. "Exactly what I expected. Nothing. Till you turned up today."

Inside the large enclosure, two tabbies were stretched out on the horizontal trunk of a dead tree. A calico was about to pounce on a leaf and rob the wind of a plaything. Three pure white Persians were eating from the same bowl and a self-satisfied Himalayan sat wrapped in its own luxurious fur coat. Luke had never seen cats in the flesh before. He couldn't see the attraction. They looked snooty and uninterested in their human visitors.

Malc scanned the area near a white post where the

wire mesh had been cut. Luke knew it would not yield any reliable information, though, because park workers had since repaired the fence and disturbed any evidence.

On the way back to the lodge, Luke said to the manager, "Do you have any poisonous animals?"

"Some, yes."

"Rattlesnakes?"

"Yes, we have a lot of rattlers. In the reptile house."

"How about eastern diamondback rattlesnakes?"

The park manager looked at Luke suspiciously. "A couple, yes."

"You've never had rattlesnakes stolen?"

"No. That would be an urgent matter for The Authorities."

"I suppose you've got handlers who'd be able to milk their venom?"

She looked even more surprised. "Just what are you investigating here?"

"Answer the question, please."

"You don't get a lot of volunteers for that – and not much need, either. My staff are keepers, not daredevils, but there are two with the necessary training. Arlene Dickinson and Tim Izzard."

"Thanks," Luke replied. "Another time, I might have a chat with them. For now, I'll work on the missing cats."

"I look forward to what you find." She said it in a

resigned tone, as if she never expected to hear from him again.

Luke opted to walk back to school. He wanted to see how easy it would be to cross unnoticed from the park.

The path through the potato fields was rough, marked by persistent lines of willowherb weeds. In the distance was the unmistakable figure of Instructor Thacket, taking a run along the walkway that, together with the cab corridor, made up the freeway. Ms Thacket was at the head of a class of students and the athletic ones were running obediently at her heels. The others were spread out behind as cabs flew past them. They were too far away for Luke to see clearly, but he guessed that the stragglers were panting painfully. They would also know there was no hope that their instructor would ease up to let them get their breath back. At this distance, they reminded Luke of mice whose only purpose was the entertainment of a sadistic cat.

Malc said, "My infrared vision indicates a warm object in the field, one hundred and seventeen metres ahead by the dry-stone wall. It is not detectable by visible light."

"What is it?" Luke asked. "Can you tell?"

"It is moving slightly so it is alive. It is a warm-blooded animal, possibly human."

"All right. Silent-mode, Malc. Go and video it."

Luke kept walking along the path as his mobile

scouted ahead. The field was very nearly flat so Luke had a clear view. In the distance, he could see the main buildings of Birmingham School. To his left and beyond the school were wind turbines. In between there was nothing but crops, genetically modified to cope with long dry periods. Even so, machines were irrigating two areas of the field by spraying great arches of water over the harvest.

In front of Malc, the head and shoulders of a boy appeared above the potato plants. He looked at Malc and, taking fright, jumped up and dashed towards the school.

Luke was almost pleased. He had been blessed with strong, long legs and he always relished a run. He took off in pursuit.

Chapter Twelve

Ahead, the distinctive boy glanced over his shoulder and saw Luke chasing him. In panic, he left the path and sprinted over the field.

Further back, but already beginning to close the gap, Luke followed suit. He scattered willowherb seeds from the edge of the path and took to the farmland. Reaching Malc's position, he said between breaths, "Go after him. Just record. Don't obstruct him unless he's getting away from me. But I'll catch him."

It wasn't an easy running surface. The crop dragged at his feet as if he were running through shallow water. He lifted his legs higher and trampled the plants as he went.

It seemed to Luke that Travis Myers was struggling even more, staggering and gasping. Luke had recognized him at once. The flaw in his genes made him stand out as the only white student. He was making for the corner of the field where the wall had collapsed, giving access to the school grounds by scrambling over the scattered stones. Keeping to a straight line, Travis went under one arch of irrigation water and almost disappeared in the mist that hung like a net curtain.

Luke stretched his legs and put on a burst of speed. Soon, he entered the artificial fog himself. With the main jet gushing over his head, every part of him was coated immediately with fine drops of water like dew. His long hair, streaming behind him, suddenly seemed heavy. His trousers soaked up the dampness and stuck to his legs. His foot caught a hidden mound of earth and he stumbled but, arms wheeling like the blades of a wind turbine, he managed to stay upright.

When he emerged from the curtain, he saw Travis looking back.

Not concentrating on where he was going, Travis lost his footing and fell. He rolled over twice and then clambered back to his feet.

Luke smiled. He was within a few metres now. Refreshed by the instant drizzle, he gulped down great mouthfuls of air and put on another spurt. He intended to bring Travis down before he reached the dry-stone wall.

His face contorted with the effort, Travis twisted and glanced back again, losing yet more speed. Unable to outrun Luke, he looked defeated already.

Luke did not even have to throw himself into a rugby tackle. He grabbed Travis by one arm and brought him to a halt twenty metres short of the illicit entrance to the school. On Luke's right, Malc hovered, recording the whole incident.

"It's over, Travis," he said. "Don't try anything else and make matters worse."

Travis could not reply right away. He put his hands on his hips and bent forward, heaving. He was exhausted and drenched.

"What was that all about?" asked Luke.

When Travis had got his breath back and straightened up, he said, "You're not going to arrest me, are you?"

"Are you going to give me a reason for arresting you?"

Travis shook his head.

"What are you doing out here?"

"I was supposed to be on a run with Ms Thacket. But. . . " He took some more breaths. "I'm not very good at it. It's torture."

"Yeah. I saw that," Luke replied. "You were hiding from her."

"And Ed Hoffman. They don't make it easy for someone like me."

Luke nodded knowingly. "Are you sure you weren't going to the animal sanctuary? Or coming back from it?"

"No. I was going to join the back of the run when they came back round again. Honest."

Luke walked completely around him, looking in particular at his pockets. "You're not carrying wire cutters?"

Puzzled, Travis frowned. "No." He patted his empty pockets.

"And you've not been near the park's cats?"

"Cats? No."

Luke looked at Malc and said, "Scan him for cat hairs."

"Already completed. None detected."

"Okay." With a grin, Luke said, "Tell me, Malc. Is avoidance of cross-country running against the law?"

"No."

"So, we don't have grounds for arresting him?"

"No."

"All right, Travis," Luke said. "You can go. Why don't you take up position over there?" He pointed to the edge of the field where it bordered the walkway. "You can join your group when they come past again. You'll get away with it because they'll think you're covered in sweat."

"You won't say anything?"

"No."

An expression of relief and gratitude appeared on Travis's face. "Oh, thank you."

Luke smiled at him. "Your trick didn't really work, though. You didn't get much of a rest. Better luck next time."

There was evidence of cats at Ms Kee's home. Every bit of wooden furniture was beautifully polished but two of the legs of her kitchen table were scratched.

"Take a look at those marks, Malc. Are they

something a cat would do?"

"That is probable. They are consistent with scratches made by cats when they sharpen their claws."

The whole place had been kept thoroughly clean, presumably to cover up any evidence of cats, but no amount of housekeeping could remove every single hair. It didn't take Luke and Malc long to find seven more. It took them longer to discover her store of food for the cats. In the kitchen, Luke noticed that one floor tile was slightly lower than the rest. Pulling it up, he found a hidden store of food underneath the floorboards.

"Even without finding a single cat," said Luke, at the end of the search, "we've got more than enough to put her at the heart of a smuggling operation. But who brought the cats to her?"

"Insufficient data."

"I tell you something else we haven't got. Flaking paint. This place is immaculate." Luke turned to Malc and said, "By now, you'll have scanned me. Do I have even one tiny cat hair on me?"

"No."

"Sawdust, paint flakes or wax? Or magnesium carbonate?"

"No."

"Well, make sure you've entered that into the files. I want it clear that I'm struggling to find any evidence against me. And re-examine every single detail of

Crispy's case. I want to know if he was in on this operation. Is there anything in there that smells remotely of cats?"

Malc answered, "We have not collected any significant data on odours."

Luke shook his head. "Who set up your language recognition programme? Whoever it was needs a good kicking."

"It was developed by an IT company and installed originally by Rick Glenfield."

"Really?"

"That was when he was an IT instructor. My programming has undergone further development and improvement since then."

"Not enough, apparently," Luke retorted. "I want you to check Crispy's details for anything that links him with cats."

"Processing."

Really, Luke was already convinced that cats would not connect the killings of Crispin Addley and Ms Kee. If Crispy had come into contact with cats, Malc would have detected it already. He would have found cat hairs on Crispy's clothes or in his quarters. Luke was merely delaying his next interview. He was putting it off for as long as possible because he was dreading it.

Luke could have got plenty of information on

rattlesnakes and their venom from Instructor Cadman but he thought that Georgia would be more friendly and open. Besides, ever since Ella Fitch had mentioned that Mr Cadman was an outstanding archer, he had become a suspect, because he was probably capable of executing the shot that had killed Crispy. Georgia Bowie was not under any suspicion so she would speak more freely. He also knew that, sooner or later, he was going to have to talk to her about pairing.

Georgia was a likeable, eye-catching girl with a great sense of fun and never-ending hair, but there was one huge problem with her. She was not Jade Vernon. It was almost painful for Luke to be with her because she reminded him of what might have been if Jade had opted for the same scientific path. If she had, Luke could have been well on the way to pairing with her by now.

Back in Year 7, he'd tried to get Jade into science by hacking into her exam scores and fiddling them, but her altered marks were so much better than Mr Cadman's expectations of her that the instructor had ordered an investigation and discovered Luke's interference. Luke's computer skills had secured his place in the line outside Ms Kee's office once again.

He was mature enough now to know that his hacking tactic wouldn't have worked anyway. Jade wouldn't have changed course for him. Her endless enthusiasm for music and fierce independence were two reasons why he loved her. But it wasn't just Jade. He was equally strong-willed. He wouldn't change his choice of career, either.

When Luke met Georgia at the reptile house in the Biology Labs, he decided to pretend that he hadn't heard about Ms Kee's intention to pair them. The subject was just too painful to raise.

Behind the glass, a warning buzz was coming from the rattler's tail. Like Luke, the snake was feeling irritable.

"I thought you had to provoke snakes quite a lot – like pick them up or stand on them – before they could be bothered to attack."

Georgia smiled and nodded. "That's right. But there are exceptions, like this one." She waved her hand towards the case containing the eastern diamondback. "It's a really bad-tempered beast. You just have to look at him a bit funny and he'll go for you. Given the chance, he'd chase you down the corridor if you made a run for it. They're very unfriendly, very poisonous."

"Do you find them in the wild?" Luke asked.

"Some rattlers are quite common down south, but not this one. They're only found in captivity – unless one or two escape, of course. Up here and further north, you don't get many rattlers in the wild, no."

"Just as well, I suppose," said Luke. "Is it easy to milk their venom?"

"Easy? No. Wearing the right gear, though, some people risk it. I once saw Mr Cadman milk one. He got it to bite on a special beaker so all the venom dribbled into it. Horrible sight. You wouldn't get me doing it, body armour or not."

Luke was beginning to take an interest in Mr Cadman. He was a good archer and he had rattlesnake venom. "Do you know anyone else who's done it?"

"They'd have to be mad, brave, suicidal or stupid." With a grin, she shook her head. "I guess the stupid ones only do it once."

Luke did not merely feel sorry for himself. He also felt sorry for Georgia. He could tell that she was wondering whether she should say anything about their likely pairing. She was probably not sure if Ms Kee's death would change anything. She might even feel threatened by his friendship with Jade but she wouldn't imagine for a moment that Luke would resist pairing. Refusals were unheard of. If Luke defied the Pairing Committee, Georgia would take it as a terrible insult. She'd done nothing to deserve that. She was really nice. Luke could never forgive himself if he hurt her. Yet he could never give up Jade.

Trying to keep his mind on the job, he asked, "Have you ever heard of an illegal trade in endangered animals — like cats?"

Georgia frowned and shook her head.

"Are there people who'd get so upset over it, they'd do anything to stop it?"

She shrugged. "The workers at the animal park, I suppose."

"No one here in school?"

"I don't know. Ask Mr Cadman. He's into that sort of thing."

"Thanks." He turned to leave, but then changed his mind. He opened his mouth to say something about their relationship but he couldn't think of anything that wasn't hurtful to her or embarrassing to him. Instead, he muttered, "See you," and walked away awkwardly.

Chapter Thirteen

It was late evening and, ignoring Malc's protests, Luke had left his mobile behind. He was sitting on the sofa with Jade in her apartment. The deep blast of sound from her speakers seemed intent on pushing them backwards against the opposite wall. When the piece ended, it left Luke breathless. "Brilliant," he cried.

"But," Jade said, turning towards him, "there's something on your mind. I can tell."

Luke thought about denying it only for a moment. There was no point because Jade would see through him. He nodded.

"These horrible murders?"

"More than that. I've just seen Georgia."

"Good."

"Good?" Luke queried.

"You've got to sort it out with her sometime. You did talk about pairing, didn't you?"

Luke hesitated.

"Typical boy!" Jade exclaimed. "Avoid the issue and hope it'll go away. Well, it won't. I'm going to have to talk to Vince. He won't go away either."

"It's okay to say we've got to talk, but what do we say?"

"We tell them the truth. What else?"

Luke shuffled uncomfortably. "And what's the truth?"

"Well, we can't do anything about the law. The law's the law. You should know that, Investigator Harding. So, like everyone else, we go along with the pairing. . . " She put up a hand to stop Luke interrupting. "We can't destroy the system but it can destroy us, so we become good citizens, but we tell Georgia and Vince that. . . well. . . you and me, we're. . . soul mates, or whatever you want to call us. We can still see each other."

"That's it, is it? You want us to be friends. Just friends."

"I didn't say that. It depends what we do when we see each other, doesn't it?"

There was disappointment in Luke's eyes as he replied, "It's not the same as being paired."

Vince was preparing for bed with a heavy cold and mixed feelings. The telescreen news had announced the death of his favourite instructor but not its cause. Around the school, everyone was muttering about another murder. Why else would Luke Harding have been summoned to her quarters? A forensic investigator would not have been called to the scene of an accident. Vince couldn't believe that she'd been killed over the theft of a few cats. He hoped not. More than that, he was desperate to believe that her fate had nothing to do with cats because, if it had, he could be next.

He left his clothes in a pile in his bedroom, sneezed violently twice, and went to the bathroom. If it weren't for Ms Kee's death, he would have been cheerful. He'd done her some favours and he was getting something in return. He had mentioned to her that he'd had his eye on Jade Vernon for some time and Ms Kee had agreed that she'd make a fine partner for him. He was sure that he would be paired with Jade when they both reached The Time. Of course, he was concerned that Ms Kee's death might untie the knot but the Chair of the Pairing Committee was so orderly and strict in everything she did that he expected her to have left instructions.

He showered away his worries and his aches and pains, and then dried himself on a big warm towel. Bent over the sink, he began to clean his teeth.

His mouth was full of foam when he heard someone burst into the room. He was so stunned that he could do nothing but straighten up. He was still holding the toothbrush in his mouth when he saw the powerful raised arm and something coming down towards him. Yanking the toothbrush out of his mouth, he was about to scream when the thing – whatever it was – exploded into his chest. The toothbrush spilled from his hand onto the floor.

To Vince, it didn't feel like a knife. That would have slid smoothly into his body. This impact was like a slow bullet. The blunt implement tore a hole in his chest, bounced off a rib and punctured his left lung which collapsed like a balloon. As he staggered back from the ferocity of the strike, the second blow shook his sternum before coming to a stop in his heart, rupturing his right ventricle and atrium. This was the fatal wound. Escaping blood filled his pericardial sac and pleural cavity. At once, Vince was seconds away from acute heart failure and inevitable death. He sucked in air frantically and then let out a dreadful cough of foam and blood.

The third stabbing caught him as he fell. The fourth and final blow landed heavily in his quietened torso as he lay on the floor, just before his eyes closed.

Luke was lying in bed, looking up at the heavens, hands behind his head. Sleep was as distant as the shining stars. Not that the night sky above him was the real thing. As usual, he'd asked Malc to project the image onto his bedroom ceiling.

He'd always had a vague memory of a crazy night before he'd started school, when he was still with his parents. That meant he would have been less than five years of age. For some long-lost reason, his mother and father had taken him and his poorly sister outdoors on a cold and clear night. Instead of sleeping in a warm and bland apartment, the four of them had spent the night in a field, wrapped up together in thick blankets. The sky had been vast and gorgeous. Luke had adored the feeling that they were being really naughty together. Yet something told him now that a great sadness had lurked behind the thrill.

Luke was the product of the pairing of an astronomer, Elisa Harding, and a doctor, Peter Sachs. Luke hoped that his parents were still alive. He had no idea where they were. His last recollections of them came from the painful time when little Kerryanne gave up her fight against disease, even before she reached school age. Luke recalled his mother's misery and his father's fury. At the time, Luke hadn't understood his father's mood but, looking back, it was simple. Peter would have been angry with himself because, as a doctor, he should have had the skill to cure his own daughter. He must have thought that he'd let her down at a ridiculously young age.

As soon as his mother and father had handed him over to the school at the age of five, he had been disconnected from his family, like every other new pupil. The Authorities had become his new parents. Luke liked to think that, one day, he'd meet his real parents again. But for now he had to be content with the calming influence of the night sky decorating his bedroom ceiling like sparkling diamonds on black cloth.

Malc's neutral voice cut through the dimness. "I detect that you are restless. Do you want me to review the case notes?"

Still motionless, dragging himself back from his mixed memories, Luke said, "Yeah, it's as good a time as any, I suppose."

In the dark, Malc was reduced to a faint flashing red light on the set of drawers to Luke's left. "At this stage, I am required to summarize. . . "

"I know. But you and me, we're going to do things a bit different. I'm going to summarize. You're going to listen and tell me if I miss anything out."

"That is an abnormal procedure but it is acceptable if I filter out any deductions that are incorrect or based on inadmissible evidence."

Beneath his miniature planetarium, Luke watched the North Star glistening on his bedroom ceiling, but seeming to be 500 light years away. That was like the solution to the two murders. The answer should be close enough to reach out and grasp but it seemed to be light years away.

"Instructor Bromley," Luke began. "Motive unknown, but he had plenty of time to shoot Crispy at four-thirty, go to the gym, take a shower and then bump into Rick Glenfield at six o'clock. He claims to be a skilled archer. And he could've passed Ms Kee – literally bumped into her – on his way to his classroom this morning. He might even have had some candle wax on his clothes, judging by all those candles in his quarters.

No known access to snake venom, though."

He paused and then continued, "Let's get it over with and do me. I've got the shooting skill and you weren't with me at the time of Crispy's murder. Our best piece of evidence — the arrow — has got my fingerprints on it. Apparently, I could have the motive of competition. But I don't. I might've wanted revenge on Ms Kee because she wasn't pairing me with Jade, and because I took a few punishments from her. I was nowhere near her when she was poisoned but you didn't have me in your sights all the time so you think I had the opportunity. It's all pure junk, of course. And I'd never ask a rattlesnake to spit in a bucket for me."

"You have included several unsubstantiated claims. Filtering."

Luke sighed and gazed at the stars for a while. "Instructor Thacket. Disliked Crispin Addley. No known alibi for four-thirty, possibly on a run. She is likely to be useful with a bow. Like almost anyone — particularly staff — she could've jabbed Ms Kee on the way into work, but no known motive and no snakes up her sleeve." Luke hurried on before Malc could object on the grounds that they had not searched in her clothing. "There are quite a few others we've barely started on — Rick Glenfield, Ella Fitch, Instructor Cadman. Mr Cadman had both weapons but no known motive. I haven't found out yet if he had the opportunity, but he teaches all about dead bodies so he's well qualified in murder. It's important to note that Rick Glenfield's got a rattlesnake. For the record, Shane's also got a fascination with snakes."

Luke's shiver could have been a lingering remembrance of that cold night spent outdoors or it could have been an after-shock of seeing the victims' bodies. "The murders aren't necessarily linked but they happened so close together, they probably are. If that's true, the use of two such different weapons is totally weird. Most killers stick to one favourite. If I can figure out why Demon Archer used an arrow and snake venom, I get a great big juicy lead. That's if Demon Archer is just one person." He took a deep breath. "What else? There's nothing to say Crispy was involved in smuggling cats but Ms Kee definitely was. That reminds me, Malc. Wherever we go and whoever we meet from now on, I want you to scan them for cat hairs."

"Logged."

"I wasn't convinced that Crispy was the intended target at first but that telescreen message suggests he was. Demon Archer knew he was having a prohibited relationship with Olivia Pang, and is smart enough to lure him out with a message that looked like it'd come from her."

Malc added, "You and Rick Glenfield would have that ability."

"And a few others, I should think. But I'm interested in the IT instructor-turned-caretaker. He acted cool about being demoted but he's feeling sore, I reckon, and his self-respect is probably rock bottom. And how about this for a theory? Glenfield goes to the firing range almost every day, according to Ella Fitch. If Crispy and Olivia used to meet there, he might have seen them together. That would lift him above me on the list of suspects because he'd know about Olivia and I didn't. He could've come up with the idea of a fake telescreen message from her and I wouldn't."

"Unproven."

"Yeah, I know. And it doesn't tell me why Glenfield would want to murder Crispy." Luke's eyes followed a meteor's streak of light across the virtual sky. "There's plenty of other little things going round up here," he said, tapping the side of his head, "but you'd say they're imagination, not fact. So, I've covered all the things you can use." He tucked his hand back behind his head. With his long black hair touching the wall, his heels overhung the bottom edge of his mattress. His height had always made him an outstanding figure at the school. "Tomorrow, I'm going to speak to Glenfield again. I want to know what he was doing before Ms Kee died. And then there's Mr Cadman, expert archer and snake-handler. It's time I leant on him."

"Physical contact is not recommended."

"Open dictionary, Malc. Lean on means put pressure on."

When Luke finally closed his eyes, it wasn't the faces of the victims or suspects that came to him this time. It wasn't even an image of little Kerryanne. He couldn't recall the baby's appearance. It was Vince Wainwright who haunted him.

Chapter Fourteen

Jade knew better than to call Luke during breakfast. His fingers and chin would be dripping with pomegranate juice and he always got annoyed at any interruption. As soon as she thought he would have finished eating, though, she established a link with Malc.

"You know I said I'd talk to Vince?" she said to him through the mobile.

"Yes?" Luke waited anxiously.

"Well, I can't," Jade replied, "because I haven't seen him around. Someone said he was coughing and spluttering with a cold but he's not even answering messages."

"That's strange."

"That's why I've told you. You're an investigator."

"All right. I'll check him out. Just don't expect me to be nice to him."

The budding architect had not locked his room. It was plastered with drawings and computer-generated plans. Mostly, Vince's sketches featured streets and structures but sometimes they portrayed people. The one that caught Luke's eye was a close-up of Jade's face. Vince had captured her warmth, her wicked smile and the endearing chaos of her hair. Tearing himself away from the drawing, Luke called out, "Vince? Hello?"

Nothing. The apartment was eerily quiet.

Luke pushed open the bedroom door but it was empty. The bed had not been slept in or maybe Vince had made it as soon as he'd got up. There was an untidy pile of clothes on a chair in the corner of the room and a pair of shoes underneath.

For some reason, Luke's heart pounded as he approached the bathroom. If Vince was still at home, he had to be inside. Gingerly, Luke slid back the door and he froze immediately with a shocked grimace on his face.

Vince was a crumpled mess on the floor by the sink. He was wearing pants and nothing else. His bare chest was blotched with blood and pink foam had solidified around his mouth. The mirror, white porcelain and tiles were spattered with deep red stains. The bathroom looked like a battlefield and on the floor lay the discarded weapon.

"Malc," Luke stammered, nodding towards the massacre.

The mobile flew over Luke's shoulder and into the bathroom while Luke stayed exactly where he was. His training told him not to encroach on the scene of the crime in case he contaminated it. Every other instinct told him to back off and run away. But a fully qualified investigator could not cave in to normal human impulses.

"There are four puncture wounds to the chest, each caused by a rounded instrument."

Luke pointed to the tool, about fifteen centimetres long and heavily bloodstained. "Like that?"

Malc scanned it. "It is consistent with the wounds."

"I can't make it out. What is it?"

"It is a glass cutter."

Luke paused and then exclaimed, "A what?"

"A glass cutter."

"You mean, one of those things with a little wheel at the end that scratches glass?"

"Correct."

"But. . . " Luke let out a long breath. "Nothing." Malc was just a machine. He was never surprised. He simply identified weapons and reported to Luke. It was left to Luke to register amazement and horror. To himself, he muttered, "Who kills with a glass cutter? Probably the same warped brain that came up with an arrow and snake venom: Demon Archer." Then he shook his head sadly. For a moment, his thoughts went back to last night. Jade had said that Vince would not go away. But now he had.

"Any prints on it?"

"None detectable, but my scan is obscured by blood."

"Vince's or someone else's as well?"

Malc did not answer right away. After analysing some of the sticky brown residue, Malc said, "I detect only one blood group. It belongs to the victim."

"Take temperatures, Malc. His body and the room. This time, there's no wind or variation to complicate things. Assume the central heating kept the bathroom at this temperature all night and he had a healthy body temperature when he was attacked. Calculate the time of death."

"It occurred between ten-thirty and midnight last night."

"While he was getting ready for bed," Luke muttered, still in the doorway. "Is that a toothbrush there? In the pool under the sink?"

"Confirmed."

"Okay. Analyse the stuff around his mouth. It's a mixture of toothpaste and blood, isn't it?"

Within a minute, Malc replied, "Correct."

Luke was beginning to overcome the shock and settle into the investigator's routine. On the wall near the mirror, there were red stains, each one like a little exclamation mark. Luke recognized the gruesome pattern. It came from the cough of someone stabbed in the chest. The splashes of blood, saliva and toothpaste had hit the tiles at an angle and tapered in the direction of the cough. He said to Malc, "Video everything – all the stains – and scan the body. Pay particular attention behind the fingernails. But I bet there's nothing there."

Completing the test, Malc stated, "I detect only soap."

Luke nodded. "He'd just had a shower, I imagine, and he was cleaning his teeth. He was so stunned when someone burst in, he didn't manage to put up a fight. He just turned towards the door, dropped his toothbrush and stood there, perfect position for being stabbed. Can you measure the wounds' entry angles?"

"Yes, but they vary. I have no way of deducing which blow was the first. Two were probably delivered while the body was falling and the final one came when the victim was on the floor. All the blows were aimed from the right so the assailant is almost certainly right-handed but I cannot estimate height. To do that, the victim would have had to stand still during the attack."

Luke let out a long breath. "Working on something like this, Malc, you must think us humans are awful."

"I am not programmed to give opinions."

"I bet there's a circuit in you somewhere that thinks you're lucky to be made of metal."

Malc replied, "Irrational. I am neither lucky nor unlucky."

Luke stepped back from the doorway. "These tiled surfaces are great for fingerprints. Do a check and throw every enhancement you've got at it." He turned his back on the room.

After a minute, Malc said, "All fingerprints belong to the victim."

"There are three footprints marked in blood. Are

they Vince's as well?"

"Confirmed."

Luke sighed. "Have you alerted The Authorities?"

"Confirmed."

Malc was about to make another observation but Luke jumped in first. "I know what you're going to say. You want me to consider the motive. This is the third one where things look bad for me."

"You requested information on both of the last two victims before they were murdered. In addition, Crispin Addley was your academic rival and Vince Wainwright was your romantic rival."

"Yes, but I was with Jade last night. She'll confirm it."

Malc said, "Her testimony would be unreliable and inadmissible."

"You mean, she'd lie because she wants Vince out of the way as well?"

"Correct."

"Look, Malc. Let's be sensible. Whoever did this went away bloodstained, possibly splattered a lot. You can test all my clothes if you like."

"I have already logged that task."

"For now," Luke said, eager for an excuse to turn his back on the bathroom, "scan the entire place, particularly the doors for fingerprints. Sample the air as well. Analyse for any foreign deodorants or other smells. And, don't forget, any evidence that I've been in here isn't significant. I'm here now. I admit it."

At the end of the process, Malc said, "Last night, you requested information on feline traces. There are fifteen cat hairs, eleven in common with those on Ms Kee's clothing."

"Ah! He was another link in the cat smuggling chain, then. Jade said he was Ms Kee's pet student. Now I know why. Tell me, have you spotted any of those fluffy willowherb seeds?"

"Yes. There is one adhering to the trousers in the bedroom and a second attached to the laces of the right shoe."

Luke nodded, feeling pleased with himself. "There was willowherb on the way to the animal sanctuary."

"I caution against deducing too much from this finding. Willowherb is not an uncommon weed. Also, when I scanned Travis Myers, I detected seeds on his trousers and trainers after he had been running in the area."

"Okay. You're equipped with a short-range X-ray probe, aren't you?"

"Confirmed."

"If you use it in here, do I have to wait outside or am I safe to stay in?"

"It is highly directional," Malc answered. "As long as you keep out of the beam, you will be safe."

"All right. Take a look around with X-rays. I'm interested in hidden metal tools."

Malc found what Luke wanted in a corner of the living room. Under the carpet and a loose floorboard, there were metal cutters and heavy pliers.

"There you are," Luke said triumphantly. "Everything you need to break into a cat compound at the animal sanctuary. He'd only need a box and he's nicely set up for lifting a few cats. So, I think we've got the boy who was spotted at the conservation park." Luke paused before adding, "Maybe the glass cutter was part of his toolset."

"What is your conclusion?"

Luke shrugged. "Only that there's a message for me here."

"Explain."

"Come on. When murderers get up in the morning they don't say, 'Off to work today. Where's my glass cutter?' They grab a knife or a gun or something. This one's really weird, even leaving the glass cutter behind to make sure I saw it. And if Demon Archer's behind all three cases, it comes after an arrow and snake venom. I don't understand the message but I know it's there – in the weapons. Every murderer has a favourite way of going about the business. Someone who kills with poison sticks with poison. No one uses an arrow, venom and a glass cutter without a very good reason. So what's the reason? What's the connection between them? Answer that and I have the message."

Chapter Fifteen

In the living room, surrounded by Vince's drawings, Luke asked, "Is there any sawdust, wax, magnesite or white paint flakes, especially on that pile of clothes in the bedroom?"

"Not on the clothes," Malc replied. "There is a fine deposit of sawdust on the carpet by the entrance. That is all."

"Show me."

"It is too small to be visible to your eyes."

Luke said, "All right. What shape is it?"

"The sawdust lies in a rough curve of 2.1 centimetres."

"So it could have fallen off a shoe?"

"That is a possibility. It cannot be linked to the intruder for certain."

"True," Luke agreed, "but is there any sawdust on Vince's shoes?"

"No," Malc answered.

"Interesting." Luke thought for a moment before saying, "You know, it's strange there's no sign of Vince's blood anywhere apart from the bathroom. The killer must have got splashed with it so there should be a trail across the floor. A drop or two at least."

"What is your conclusion?"

"Well, whoever did it could've put on a waterproof overall – something like plastic or nylon – while Vince was in the shower. After the stabbing, Demon Archer could have washed it down in the shower and flushed all the blood away. Or wrapped it up, taken it somewhere and destroyed it. He – or she, I suppose – could've just brought a spare set of clothes." Again, Luke paused. "Of course, no one would take any particular notice of a caretaker or technician wandering around in overalls or carrying a bin bag."

"Do you have such an overall?"

"Me? No," Luke answered with frustration in his voice. "Let's keep to the point. Would I be right in thinking you'd need to be pretty strong to stab someone that thoroughly with a glass cutter? It's nowhere near as sharp as a knife."

"I cannot measure the force used without the results from a post-mortem but the attack would require considerable power."

"Like a man or an athletic woman. Like the strength needed to make the shot that got Crispy."

"That is probable."

"Tell me about fingerprints."

"Fingerprints are the unique patterns left behind. . ."

"No," said Luke. "I mean, tell me what you've found here."

"Over ninety-five per cent of the fingerprints are

119

those of the victim. I have not yet assigned the others to individuals with the exception of. . . ”

"Yes, yes," Luke interrupted. "Apart from mine."

"Correct. However, yours may be the result of this visit."

"Nice of you to say so."

"It is unlikely that fingerprint evidence will be helpful because only yours and the victim's appear on the bathroom door. If another person opened the door, he or she must have been wearing gloves."

"Okay, Malc," Luke said. "Let's wrap it up here."

"Explain."

"Finish off. Call in the pathologist's team and then seal the apartment. I've got to go to Jade and tell her what's happened. Then it's on with the case. Glenfield and Cadman."

Amazingly, after three days, Jade was still blonde. She hadn't yet got bored with her appearance and changed it once more. "Hiya," she said brightly. But when she saw Luke's expression, she began to frown. "What's happened?"

"It's Vince."

"What do you mean?" she muttered.

Luke looked at her but the words didn't come to him.

"No, not another one! But. . . that's terrible. He

was. . ." She shook her head.

Luke put his arms around her.

They stood there in the music studio for several minutes, neither daring to say anything. It would have been tactless to give vent to any feelings apart from the dismay of Vince's death. When a boy's life had been snatched away, they couldn't allow themselves to think about the consequences for their own relationship.

Eventually, Luke pulled back. "Keep quiet about it for the moment, Jade." Then, reluctantly, he added, "I'm sorry but, for the record, you've got to tell Malc what you were doing and where you were last night between ten-thirty and twelve."

"What?" Jade exclaimed.

"Sorry," he repeated.

"Someone's dead and all you can do is ask questions."

He nodded sadly. "That's my job."

Jade was getting angry. "Do you suspect me? How could you?"

Luke shook his head. "No. Of course not. It's just that your answer might help another suspect."

Jade frowned, hesitated, and then said, "Oh, I see. You mean you."

"Yes. But I can't lead you to the answer. I've got to have it in your own words. Malc isn't programmed to believe you anyway, but I still want what you've got to say on record."

She glared at the robot and said, "He was with me, in my quarters. All the time."

Malc accepted the statement in silence but he would not add it to the case notes.

Rick Glenfield was painting the doorframe in the old kitchen that he was helping to convert into a maths classroom. He was wearing worn and stained denim. With that mass of ginger hair, simple face and dumpy body, he reminded Luke of a teddy bear.

Luke looked at him and smiled. "Messy job."

Suspiciously, Rick answered, "Yes."

"Doesn't the school give you some sort of overall?"

"Yes. But. . . er. . . I tore it yesterday and had to bin it. I'm waiting for a new one."

"Tore it?" Luke replied. "How come?"

"A door handle. This one to be precise. I walked through the door and my pocket caught on it. There was a big rip, like thunder. I came through but a lot of the overall didn't."

"It couldn't have been very strong. What was it made of?"

The caretaker frowned. "Nylon."

Realizing that Rick was getting cagey about his interest in work clothes, Luke moved on. "Have you ever milked the venom from a rattler?"

Ill at ease, Rick laughed weakly. "No. I wouldn't fancy

my chances." He stopped painting but kept the brush in his right hand.

"Were you out last night?"

"No," Rick replied. "I used to socialize quite a lot but not these days. It's not easy, you know. I used to mix with the instructors but I'm not one of them now. They're awkward with me because they don't how to react. But the non-teaching staff still think of me as an instructor. I'm. . . neither one thing nor the other. A fish out of water either way. So, I keep myself to myself. Besides, after Ms Kee and all, I didn't feel like it."

Luke looked around the classroom. Behind Rick, there were three rows of tables. They weren't new but they had been smartened up, ready for use. "Big job, this. Have you been on it for a while?"

"On and off. It's not all I do but, yes, I've got my work cut out."

"You were working here the day before yesterday, then?"

"Not all day, but yes. Ms Kee sent me some students who'd misbehaved." After mentioning the deputy head again, he shook his head sadly. "They did half an hour's work in here after school as punishment. More trouble than a help to me, to be honest."

"Who were they?"

Rick shrugged. "I didn't take names. Ms Kee'll have them." He hesitated before adding, "Sorry. I mean, I

suppose she'll have left a record if you want to know." Then he looked into Luke's face and said, "Before you graduated, you would've been on the list. You were no angel."

Luke nodded. "You remember me hacking into the exam scores."

Rick looked away as if unwilling to think about it. Shutting down like a clam, he muttered, "Yes."

"There was a loophole in the programme that allowed me to sneak in."

"I know."

In an attempt to get Rick to open up again, Luke asked, "I got into deep trouble for it. Did you as well?"

Rick turned away as if he needed to compose himself before answering. Apparently unable to face Luke any more, he dipped his brush into the paint and slapped it onto the wood violently. "You're not kidding. I got blamed, yes," he said through gritted teeth.

"Sorry about that. You shouldn't have done. You only installed it. It was me that broke into it."

"It's too late for apologies," Rick snapped, spreading the paint over the doorframe with his back to Luke.

"Well, thanks. You've been very helpful."

"Have I?"

"Oh yes," Luke replied.

Chapter Sixteen

"Cat hairs?" Luke enquired, as he walked away from the messy room where Rick Glenfield was working.

"What do you want to know about them?"

"You scanned Glenfield. Did you find any?"

"No. Nor did I find any on Jade Vernon."

"You scanned Jade?" Luke exclaimed.

"You ordered me to scan everyone."

Luke sighed. "Yes. I guess I did. But Jade. . . never mind. Did you find any white paint flakes on Glenfield?"

"Most of the paint stains on the denim shirt were fresh smears but there were two fragments of old white paint, identical to that found on Ms Kee's clothing."

"Now that's interesting. Not a killer punch, though. It might mean they've both been in the same place, that's all. Maybe she walked her bad boys and girls down to the old kitchen for that detention. She could've come into contact with the old paint there. Was there any sawdust on him?"

"Yes. Traces adhering to the trousers. I cannot tell if it matches the samples from Ms Kee or Vince Wainwright's room."

"Any mystery wax or magnesium carbonate?"

Malc answered, "There was none on the exposed skin

and clothing that I could scan."

"Okay. I'm authorizing you to monitor the use of his identity card. If he leaves school, I want to know. If he takes a cab, I want you to register his destination and tell me."

"Logged."

"And send an order to intercept his rubbish. I want to see the big rip he claims is in his overalls."

"Order sent."

Luke stopped outside Ms Kee's office. Filling the corridor with fragrance, a bouquet of lilies from the greenhouse had been left by her door as a reminder and a tribute. A new deputy head had not yet been appointed to take over her job so the room was unoccupied. Luke swiped his card past the security pad and the door clicked open. Inside, he sat at her desk and turned on her computer. "Malc, establish a radio link with her system and interrogate it for a list of students she put in detention on Tuesday afternoon. They could all have it in for her."

"Four pupils were punished by her within the parameters you set."

"Any familiar names?"

"Yes."

"And?" Luke prompted.

"What is your enquiry?" asked Malc.

"Give me the familiar names."

"Ed Hoffman was disciplined for bullying on Tuesday morning."

Luke nodded. "Do any of the other three have anything to do with Crispy or Vince?"

"Unlikely. They were all students from Year 8."

"Any connections with snakes?"

"None on record."

Pushing his luck, Luke said, "While you're linked, Malc, do a search for any documents that mention cats, snakes, arrows, archery, or glass cutters."

Thirty seconds later, Malc replied, "There are many references to archery and arrows. All relate to legitimate sports usage and lessons. There are no other relevant files for those search terms."

FI Harding had the authority to drag an instructor out of a lesson if he thought that an immediate interview would advance a case. He decided to use that authority to speak to Mr Cadman.

Before the science instructor left his class, he told his students how they should continue the lesson in his absence. Then, as always, he grabbed his sunglasses and hat. Outside the classroom, he wore sunglasses and a rimmed hat almost all of the time. He also seemed to wear a smart fresh suit every single day of the week. As a result, he had a reputation for being smooth. Unusually for a scientist, he adored jazz.

Luke took him to the edge of the school fields and sat down on a bench. Malc parked himself on the grass a metre in front of them, recording their exchange.

Guessing what Luke was about to ask, Instructor Cadman said, "Crispin Addley was the ideal student. Not as naturally gifted as some," he said, looking sideways at Luke, "but clever, eager to learn, and respectful." The shadow from the rim of his hat fell over his eyes, already hidden by sunglasses.

"So, you got on well with him?"

"Very."

Trying to spring a surprise, Luke said, "Have you ever milked the venom from a rattlesnake?"

With barely a pause, Mr Cadman chuckled. "Excellent. I can see you've remembered your training."

"What do you mean?"

"I'm sure you've already got the answer from one of my students but you still ask the question. That way, when I deny it, you know I'm lying. You know I'm covering something up. But I don't deny it."

Mr Cadman was not just smooth. He also had a reputation for being sharp. It didn't bother Luke. In practice interviews, he'd discovered that the clever ones were sometimes so sure of their superiority that they couldn't imagine making a slip or getting caught. Luke hoped he was smart enough to exploit that arrogance. "Okay," he said. "I'll ask something I don't know about you. Are you any good at archery?"

"So-so."

"So-so?"

Mr Cadman shrugged. "Maybe a bit more than so-so."

Luke guessed that Mr Cadman was being modest rather than dishonest but it was hard to tell without seeing his eyes. Luke got a good view only of the instructor's nose, cheeks and mouth with its superbly trimmed moustache.

The field was marked out with pitches of different sizes and shapes. From the bench, Luke could see ongoing games of baseball and football. Less frequently than usual, the coaches shouted instructions at players. Nearer, a student accelerated down the track, took off and landed untidily in a shower of sand. Other pupils waited in a short queue while an instructor adjusted the high-jump bar unenthusiastically. Luke glanced beyond the pitches and tracks towards the firing range. It was out of sight because the ground sloped up slightly to a crown and then fell away to the spot where archers practised. From the bench, he could see the blades of the wind farm waving above the mound and the distant tops of trees shedding dry yellowy leaves.

The whole games area was much less lively than normal. The first two deaths were souring the atmosphere of the school. Luke hadn't announced the third yet. He hoped that a suspect might reveal knowledge of Vince Wainwright's murder before he put out a statement. That would be incriminating, but not proof of guilt. When people noticed that Vince's room had been sealed and that he was not in lessons, rumours would soon start to fly. Probably, they were flying already.

"What did you do with the snake venom?"

"More training tactics. Confuse the suspect by switching subjects."

Luke stared at him, waiting for a reply.

"I destroyed it. It was just an exercise – to show the students how it's done."

"Does that mean they could all do it?"

Mr Cadman laughed. "When I showed you how to conduct a post mortem, I didn't expect you to pick up a scalpel and do it yourself. But you had to know what happens."

"Who have you trained to do it?"

"No one in school."

"Out of school?"

"I've helped the animal sanctuary once or twice," Mr Cadman answered. "It's not a regular thing."

"Apart from the people at the animal sanctuary, who would you say is capable of milking snake venom?"

Mr Cadman thought about it for a moment. "I can't say I know anyone but me."

Luke looked at Mr Cadman's immaculate suit and

decided that Malc would not spot a single hair on it. He decided to ask about cats instead. "Do you have an interest in cats?"

"Yes."

"And what sort of interest is that?"

Mr Cadman shrugged. "I'm a biologist. I'm fascinated by all creatures great and small."

"If you've got contacts with the conservation park, you'll know about their cat smuggling problem."

"I do, yes. And I'm appalled by it."

Luke looked out in the direction of the sanctuary and then back at Instructor Cadman. "Do you know who's behind it?"

"There's been rumours for ages it's going on in school. I don't know. But if I did, I'd. . . " The biologist shook his head. The taut lips under his moustache suggested anger.

"You'd what?"

"I'd give them a piece of my mind. Endangered species aren't suitable as pets."

"Do you know anyone who'd go further to stop it?"

Behind his sunglasses, Mr Cadman stared at Luke. "Are you saying Crispin Addley and Ms Kee were involved?"

Luke shook his head. "I'm just asking questions. And I require answers." Of course, Mr Cadman could be playing a game. He might know perfectly well that Ms

Kee was at the heart of an illicit trade in endangered cats. Not mentioning Vince Wainwright could be part of the same game, with the intention of suggesting that he didn't know the student had been murdered last night.

"People can get upset about animals – more upset about them than humans – but such people love living things. They wouldn't kill anything – or anyone."

Luke was not convinced. In his mind, he'd already placed Mr Cadman high on his list of suspects because he had a strong motive for removing Ms Kee and Vince from the smuggling chain. If Cadman thought that Crispy was another link, the instructor would be at the top of Luke's list. "Were you on the firing range after school on Tuesday?"

"No. I was marking students' work."

"On your own?"

Mr Cadman's lips curved into a dry smile. "Yes. There's no one to vouch for me, I'm afraid."

"And where were you last night?"

"Last night? In my quarters, listening to a documentary on jazz."

"Jazz? What aspect of jazz?"

"You were trained well, weren't you? It was on female singers."

"Did you see Ms Kee yesterday morning, before school?"

"So I could poison her with snake venom? No."

Before Malc could intervene, Luke said, "I haven't released a statement on the cause of Ms Kee's death."

Mr Cadman laughed again. "I don't need a statement. Crispin Addley was shot with an arrow and you asked about archery. Ms Kee died and you're very keen to ask about rattler venom. It doesn't take a genius."

"Rick Glenfield keeps snakes. Has he ever had training or advice from you?"

"He asked about cage conditions once, as I recall. No more than that. He doesn't say much. Especially not to me."

"Why not?" asked Luke.

Mr Cadman adjusted his hat to block out more of the dazzling sun, low in the sky. "As part of my job in Biology, I do a lot of computing, so I took over some of his duties in general IT."

On the field, a student cursed loudly as he brought down the high-jump bar with a trailing heel. A bunch of Year-9 pupils pounded around the running track for the third time. To Luke's right, a hose was spraying water onto the parched turf. Strong sunlight caught the droplets and formed a mini-rainbow.

Luke decided he wasn't going to get any more for the moment so he stood up. "What do you do when you're not teaching, shooting or listening to jazz?"

For the first time, Mr Cadman became defensive. "I'm not the only one who relaxes with archery – and music. It wasn't long ago that you had a hobby of shooting. And you did it very well, much to the annoyance of the sporty types." Then he got to his feet and lifted his hat in a mock gesture of parting. "When I have a bit of spare time, I collect hats and antique furniture."

Chapter Seventeen

As they left the breezy field, Malc announced, "A nylon overall has been recovered from Rick Glenfield's waste and delivered to your quarters."

Luke smiled. "Let's go and take a look. I just love going through other people's rubbish."

Unable to hear the sarcasm in Luke's voice, Malc replied, "Most forensic investigators find it beneficial."

"Mmm. What about your second check on whether there's anything that links Crispy to cats?" said Luke as he strode quickly towards the block of apartments. "What's the answer?"

"I find no connection."

"So, Crispy's the odd one out," Luke said to himself. "Cadman's got no obvious motive for killing him."

"There is only one suspect with a motive for all three victims," Malc added.

"Yes. Thanks for that," Luke retorted. "Just tell me. Was there a programme on female jazz singers last night and what time was it?"

"Confirmed. It was transmitted between ten o'clock and eleven."

"Not exactly a perfect alibi, is it? No one to back him up and, when he'd finished watching, he still had time to get to Vince's quarters with a glass cutter."

"The pathologist has now established that the glass cutter was the weapon that caused Vince Wainwright's wounds. It too has been delivered to your quarters."

"Good."

Luke passed his identity card through the outer security panel of the accommodation block and the door unlocked for him. "I hope you've noted another important fact about Mr Cadman, Malc. He's into antique furniture."

Malc hesitated. "He did not testify to getting inside."

"No. I mean he collects it."

"Explain the significance."

"I'm sure he's no stranger to wax polish."

"Tenuous, but logged," Malc replied.

Inside his apartment, Luke spread out and examined Rick Glenfield's overall. There was a rip from the shoulder to the pocket, just as Rick had claimed. Malc scanned the garment, searching for the telltale spectra of haemoglobin or blood proteins, but could not detect any among the smears of workplace dirt and contamination from the trash pile.

"Are there any viruses on it, Malc? According to Jade, Vince had a cold. When he coughed up blood, he'd splatter germs around as well."

Malc tested the overall again and then reported, "None detected."

"Okay. There's nothing to say this is Demon Archer's

so I'll tell you what we do. You put an order out to have all rubbish searched. And I mean all. Every single bin on site. I'm looking for bloodstained clothes. Or a syringe with Ms Kee's blood at one end and Demon Archer's fingerprints at the other. That'd go down very well."

"Order sent."

"And talking of clothes, Malc. . . " Luke went to his own wardrobe, opened the door and, with an exaggerated sweep of his arm, invited Malc to scan inside. "If you find any sign of blood on mine, I'll walk to Cambridge and volunteer to lock myself in prison."

Malc's spectroscopic examination failed to pick out specks of blood. Determined to be thorough, he tried a more sensitive method. He released phthaldialdehyde into the wardrobe and then swept intense ultraviolet light across the clothes to pick out shiny spots that the reagent would create if it came into contact with blood proteins. Three minutes later, he said, "I have detected one tiny blood stain on the sleeve of a jumper. The blood group indicates that it is your own blood."

"I cut my hand a while back. None of Vince's?"

"No."

"Admit it," Luke said with a grin. "You're struggling to find one vital piece of evidence against me."

"This morning, you reasoned that Demon Archer could have washed an overall in the shower or destroyed either the overall or a spare set of clothes. This speculation also applies to you. As for crucial evidence, we have your fingerprints on the arrow."

Luke did not reply. He was still troubled by the finding of his prints on one of the murder weapons. He took the bag containing the glass cutter and dangled it in midair so that Malc could sweep all the way around it. "Any fingerprints this time?" he asked. He felt nervous in case his prints turned up again even though he had never held a glass cutter in his bare hand.

"No."

Luke sighed with relief. To make it seem that he was only thinking about somebody else's prints, he said, "I'd have been amazed if there was. One thing's for sure, we're not dealing with a fool. Any markings to identify it?"

"None."

"Check the school computer. Has anyone ordered a glass cutter recently?"

"No."

"It's probably been pinched from a workshop or bought outside school. Maybe by Vince. Anyway, it'll be impossible to trace."

Shaking his head, Luke looked in turn at the murder weapons and muttered to himself, "An arrow and a glass cutter. And snake venom. The answer's right here."

In her apartment, Olivia Pang sat in the same crumpled

clothes. Luke guessed that Crispy's illicit girlfriend had hardly moved for two days. "How are you doing?" he asked needlessly. He could see that she was suffering beyond words.

Olivia looked up at Malc and then said to Luke, "Official visit this time?"

"I have to ask you something for the record. It's not about your friendship with Crispy."

Olivia lowered her bloodshot eyes and waited.

"Did he have anything to do with cats, Olivia?"

Frowning, she looked up again. "Cats?"

"Yes."

She shook her head. "No."

"Are you absolutely sure?"

"Yes," she mumbled.

"Could he have kept it from you?"

"We told each other everything."

"How about cat smuggling?"

"No," she answered, on the verge of sobbing once more.

"Bear with me, Olivia. I'm trying to help him – and you. If Crispy knew someone was planning to do something violent – for instance, to stop a cat smuggling operation – would he have tried to report it or get in the way? I ask because he might've made himself an enemy that way."

"Yes, he would've tried to do something about it," she

replied. "He was like that. He didn't like violence."

"What he planned would've been dangerous so he might have kept it to himself to protect you. What do you think?"

Olivia let out a long sigh. "I think he would've told me," she insisted.

"One final thing," said Luke. "When you were with Crispy, were you ever spotted by the caretaker? You know, Rick Glenfield."

Olivia shrugged. "Not as far as I know."

"How about Mr Cadman? Did he know about the two of you?"

"Mr Cadman? I don't see how he would."

"Did Crispy get on all right with him?"

Surprised, Olivia looked at Luke full in the face. "He was Crispy's favourite."

It was after lunch when Luke caught up with Ed Hoffman in the gym. Ed's sporting pedigree was flawless. Descended from generations of elite athletes, he had wide shoulders, a short muscular neck, bulging arms and powerfully built legs. The swagger of his brawny body also spilled over into his manner. He was a vindictive and arrogant bully.

"You and me," Luke began, "have a history. I have to say that for the record." He glanced towards Malc.

Ed stood with a basketball wedged between his hand

and thigh. "What do you want?"

"I'm told you were caught bullying on Tuesday morning and got detention for it in the afternoon. Punishing you was one of the last things Ms Kee did."

Ed shrugged. "I wasn't the only one."

"No," Luke admitted. "I've got a list, but you're the one I'm interested in. It wasn't the first time she'd had a go at you."

Ed was shorter than Luke but much more beefy. He let out a grunt. "She caught you as much as me."

"True." Everyone was taught from an early age to trust mobile aids to law and crime because they always spoke the truth, so Luke turned to Malc and asked, "Am I on your list of suspects for the murder of Ms Kee?"

"Confirmed."

Ed laughed. It was a deep rumbling sound, filled with malice. "You're investigating yourself! Can't wait for you to charge yourself with murder." He bounced the basketball twice and then threw it half the length of the court. It dropped through the hoop and net without even striking the backboard.

"Good shot."

Not responding to the compliment, Ed repeated, "What do you want, Harding?"

Ignoring his question, Luke said, "You were always good at games. Any games. Even computer games."

"So what?"

"I seem to remember you were into computers back then."

"Huh. I prefer this." Ed nodded at the court.

"I really wanted to ask what you did in that detention."

"Sanded down table tops."

"To take off peeling paint?"

"Yeah."

"What colour was it?"

"White," Ed answered. "So what?"

"Did Ms Kee send you down to the room or take you herself?"

"Does it matter?"

Luke said, "Yes. Answer the question, please."

"She told us to report to the old kitchen. Said the caretaker would be there."

"Did you see Ms Kee yesterday, first thing?"

"No. I was with my mates."

Luke smiled. He didn't doubt for a moment that Ed could find any number of students who'd back up every word he said. If they didn't do it willingly, Ed would provide a powerful incentive, no doubt. Luke watched him carefully as he asked, "Ever heard of *Crotalus adamanteus*?"

"What? When they taught you criminology," he said in his gruff voice, "did they make you speak funny as well?"

"What did you do straight after that detention on Tuesday?"

"What do you think? I went across the field and shot Crispin Addley."

Turning to Malc, Luke said, "For the record, that's not a confession. It's an attempt to provoke me. And a way of telling me not to be ridiculous." Facing Ed again, he asked, "What did you do really?"

"I was with my mates."

"Them again," Luke muttered. "How about last night?"

"Same thing. Same mates."

"I've seen your archery scores on your computer record. They're. . . okay, but they stop about a year ago."

"Because I stopped doing it. Obviously."

"Why?"

"Better things to do with my time. Like basketball, weightlifting and baseball."

Luke decided to introduce a fantasy to see Ed's reaction. Hoping that Malc would not correct him, he said, "But I've spoken to people who've seen you on the firing range."

"Did you test their eyesight?" Ed retorted.

"Have you been practising?"

Ed shrugged again. "Not really. Maybe two or three times in the last year. Not enough to be the best and, if I'm not the best, I'm not interested."

"Do you like cats?"

Revelling in his crazy tough-guy image, Ed replied, "They're great with chips and carrots."

Luke had to smile but the forensic investigator within him had to keep it official. "Are you saying you haven't come into contact with any cats?" Nodding towards Malc, Luke added, "Remember, I will check."

"Oh, I'm scared." Ed paused and then said, "No, I haven't. I don't know what you're talking about."

"How about snakes, then? They're more your sort of thing."

"Yeah. I like the way they move and eat things whole — like cats."

"Do you keep any snakes?" Luke asked.

"No. Look, I don't know about these stupid questions. If I'd murdered someone, you'd know about it. I'd batter them to death with a baseball bat. Or spear them with a javelin. No messing."

Luke was getting nowhere. He was establishing only that he would never be a friend of Ed Hoffman. He would always regard Hoffman as a nasty spiteful character, best avoided. But that wasn't enough to make him a significant suspect. "That's it," Luke said. "For now anyway."

Ed walked over to the stand where the barbells were stored. Before he chose the weight he wanted to lift, he dunked his hands in chalk to improve his grip. When he clapped his hands gently to remove the surplus, he created a miniature white cloud. "You know, Harding," he said, "I agree with you about one thing. You and me sure do have a history. One day, I'll bury a javelin in your chest." He looked deadly serious for a moment but then a broad grin spread across his face. An unpleasant grin.

Luke walked away. He couldn't say sorry to Ed for the incident with the javelin because he wasn't.

In the changing rooms, Malc scanned inside Ed's locker. There were no traces of cat hairs, paint, sawdust or wax on his newly laundered clothes but two willowherb seeds were clinging to his shoes.

Chapter Eighteen

After school had finished for the day, Luke went back to the kitchen that was being redecorated. In the deserted room, he dragged the tip of his forefinger across a windowsill and examined the grey stain. "Sawdust. When Ed Hoffman left here, he'd have been covered in it." He told Malc to do a complete scan of the room and, as he expected, his mobile found several white paint flakes and a faint layer of sawdust.

Luke kicked at the bare concrete floor with his shoe. "You said magnesite was made into non-slip concrete floors for kitchens. Is that what this is?"

"No. It is standard concrete."

"Oh." Malc's answer was not what Luke had expected. "Never mind," he said, "I want you to analyse those table tops now and tell me how they've been treated."

"They have been coated with wax polish."

This time Luke was not surprised. "Is it the same wax you found on Ms Kee?"

"Comparison is not possible because the sample on her clothing was too small."

"You must have got some sort of infrared signature from it."

"Yes, but it was a very weak signal. In addition, all

waxes have very similar infrared spectra. They are not distinctive."

"Pity." Luke paused for a moment and then said, "By the way, you must have scanned Olivia and her room for cat hairs. Any joy?"

"I do not experience joy and I did not detect any feline matter."

Malc was not just a Mobile Aid to Law and Crime. He was also a sophisticated communications device. The voice that began to boom out of him wasn't his normal way of talking. Luke recognized the unmistakable bossy tone even before the speaker introduced himself as a spokesman for The Authorities.

"We are concerned, FI Harding. This case has become more complex than we anticipated for your first assignment. There is also the unfortunate difficulty that you have become a strong suspect."

Perturbed by the sudden intrusion, Luke swallowed. "Are you worried I might not solve it before another death?" That was exactly what was worrying him.

"We are confident in your prospects as a forensic investigator but we were hoping for more progress."

"Some things are falling into place now. I'm getting there."

The spokesman hesitated before replying, "We can relieve you of the responsibility without a blemish on your profile. It is not your fault that it has become complicated. There is no disgrace in requesting a simpler case at this stage. We can hand it over to a more experienced investigator."

Luke felt like a pupil who'd turned in a poor set of marks. But he was also very determined. "I'm not asking for something easier. I'm not stuck and I've got some good leads. I will solve it." For Luke, failing was unthinkable.

There was another delay. "You have two more days. Then we will assess your progress. If, in the meantime, you want to be transferred to a different case, simply request it through your mobile. You may keep your accommodation in school until you solve the case or you are relieved of it. For now, continue, FI Harding."

There was only one person to go and see when he felt depressed. He always found Jade's enthusiasm infectious.

"Hiya," she said. "Listen. I know you haven't got time but you have just got to hear this."

"Hear what?"

"Stay right where you are, Investigator Harding. Don't move!"

Luke stood there, watching her direct some sort of probe towards him, like the barrel of a gun.

"Okay," Jade said. "I'm going to turn it on. You'll hear some music."

Luke braced himself but this time it wasn't an ordeal. It was merely a repeating riff played on an acoustic guitar. "Yes. It's nice but. . . so what?"

"Take one step to the left."

As he moved, the music faded to nothing. He looked up at Jade in surprise. "It's gone."

Jade was beaming with pleasure at his astonishment. "Go back to where you were."

"It's back again!"

"I know," Jade replied. "Now take a step to the right."

The same thing happened again. The guitar chords were suddenly out of his earshot. "That's amazing," said Luke.

Jade nodded. "It's a thin beam of music. Right now it's going past your shoulder. I'm going to call it spotlight sound because I can direct it like a spotlight. Brilliant. Lots of people have tried to get to grips with something like this but I'm the only one who's actually done it."

Silent, Luke shivered.

"What's wrong?" Jade asked him.

"Nothing. Absolutely nothing." A grin began to grow slowly around his lips. "Say that again."

"What?"

"What you just said."

While Jade thought about it, Malc interrupted. "I have her words in my memory. . . "

Luke put up his hand. "No. I want to hear Jade."

"Er. . . lots of people have tried to get to grips with spotlight sound but I'm the only one who's done it."

Luke nodded as the full-blown grin finally arrived on his face. Forgetting that Malc was still in record mode, he went up to Jade and kissed her on the mouth. "You're a genius."

Jade smiled. "I know."

Luke clutched her arm briefly and said, "Thanks. I've got to go."

As Luke walked away, Jade called after him, "Hey, what did you come for?"

Over his shoulder, he answered, "Inspiration."

Chapter Nineteen

Malc said, "Your behaviour is beyond normal parameters. Explain."

Dashing towards his quarters, Luke laughed. "Don't panic. Let's get back first, then I'll tell you."

Inside his apartment, Luke sat at his desk, closed his eyes for a few seconds and then sighed with pleasure. He took the arrow that killed Crispin Addley, holding it by its transparent protective sleeve, and said to Malc, "Something's been bugging me about these prints. Now I know what it is, courtesy of Jade. 'Lots of people have tried to get to grips with something like this but I'm the only one who's done it,' she said."

"Explain."

"How many prints are there on the shaft?"

"Two," Malc answered. "Both are yours. A thumb and forefinger."

"Don't you see? All the other arrows in the weapons store were plastered with fingerprints. Lots of people got to grips with them but apparently I'm the only one who's touched this one. To quote you, Malc, that's illogical. It must have been used by lots of people, especially students. So why only one person's prints?"

"What is your conclusion?"

"It's all been planned very carefully. Someone wiped the arrow clean, made sure I used it for target practice – or maybe in that competition – and then stored it, ready for murdering Crispy. Demon Archer only had to use gloves to make it look like I killed him. I've been set up!"

"Unproven, but it is a possibility."

"A strong possibility. You said the prints were weak. That's because they're not fresh. They've been there for ages!"

"Speculation."

Ignoring him, Luke said, "This changes everything, especially the motive. Who'd want to nobble me? Shane maybe. Remember? He bore me a grudge. Ed Hoffman – definitely in the frame now. Ms Thacket, because I abandoned sport. And perhaps Rick Glenfield. He got into big trouble because of me. I might've upset others. I don't know."

"You must not discount the other active leads at this stage."

"I'm not. I'm just following the most likely one. Get your logic circuits flying, Malc. I've been working on motives for killing Crispy, Ms Kee and Vince. But that's not the point. The victims could've been chosen just to make me look guilty. It might have been nothing to do with them. It was their bad luck to have a gripe with me, that's all. No wonder I've been struggling over a motive for Crispy's murder. Maybe there wasn't one.

Not really."

"That is not the only theory," Malc commented dryly and accurately.

Luke put down the arrow and felt yet another tingle in his spine. "Malc, there's something else. What's a fingerprint?"

"It is a unique pattern. . . "

"No, I mean, what is it chemically? What's the pattern made of?"

"It is a greasy secretion from skin called sebum, with salt, amino acids, urea. . . "

"Exactly. The fatty stuff from an adult lasts for months, if not years, yes?"

"Correct."

"But a child hardly makes a mark. Its fingerprints disappear in hours."

"Confirmed. A child's sebaceous glands produce very little sebum."

"So, what about mine? What about a sixteen-year-old boy, Malc?"

"After puberty, a fingerprint persists almost as much as an adult's."

"That's what I thought. My fingerprints could have got on the arrow weeks, maybe months, ago."

"That is a possibility."

"We can check," Luke said.

"How?"

Luke stood up. "It's time to see Ella Fitch again."

They found the technician on the balcony of The Great Hall. She was rigging up the lighting in the huge room ready for Ms Kee's memorial service on Saturday. The event was going to be a celebration of the deputy head's life and The Authorities had decided that everyone in the school would be present. Ella was making sure that the spotlights would pick out the head, a dignitary from The Authorities, and one of Ms Kee's colleagues who would come to the front of the stage to say a few words about her.

Ella didn't need a question to set her off. As soon as she saw Luke, she said, "Ah, the diamond investigator. Have I heard it right? You've sealed Vince Wainwright's room. Does that mean there's been another murder?"

"Vince's room is a restricted crime scene," Luke replied. "But that's all I'm saying at the moment." To distract her from Vince, Luke nodded towards the hall, spread out below them, and said, "I didn't know you'd be asked to set this up."

"It's not just me. Your — how shall I put it? — your friend's going to sort out the music for the occasion."

"Jade."

With something like a smirk on her face, Ella said, "Yes."

Luke was realizing that Ella soaked up information

and rumour like a sponge. She knew about the cat smuggling, she knew the best archers, she knew – probably before Jade herself – that Jade would be enlisted to provide appropriate music for the memorial, and she knew that he had an unwise relationship with Jade. Moving her on to a less awkward topic again, he said, "I meant to ask you. Are you missing any tools?"

"Tools?"

"Yes. Any sort of tools."

"I don't think so. No. Not that I've noticed, anyway. What have you got in mind?"

Luke would not give even the slightest hint that he was interested in a glass cutter. The cause of Ms Kee's murder had got out, but he would keep secret the way that Vince had died. Then, if a suspect knew about the glass cutter, Luke had positive proof of guilt. "It doesn't matter," he said. "It's not important. The other thing I wanted to say was about that javelin."

"So, you *are* investigating horrible Hoffman. Fruity."

"I just wanted to see it, that's all. You said you'd kept it."

"That's right."

"Did anyone else touch it after you and me?" asked Luke. "No."

"Where is it?"

"In the rack in my workshop. I'll come and show you right now if you like. Anything to help out."

"It's all right. You look busy here." He extracted his

identity card and waved it towards her. "I can get in. You don't mind me poking around, do you?" His tone suggested that he'd regard a refusal as suspicious.

Ella hesitated for a fraction of a second but she shrugged and said, "Help yourself."

Heading across the courtyard towards the workshop with Luke, Malc said, "I did not detect cat hairs on Ella Fitch."

Luke was not very interested. He was following a different lead now. "I didn't think you would."

Inside Ella's working area, there was a large cupboard. When Luke folded back its doors, he revealed a store for equipment that was waiting for repair or maintenance. In the rack, there were two javelins. He could not remember which one he had sabotaged at the sports day just over a year ago. Even so, the javelins brought memories flooding back to him. The school had required every student to perform in at least one event of the games and Luke had chosen the archery competition.

"Malc, scan both javelins for my prints."

"They appear on the left-hand javelin only."

Luke nodded, walked up to the one on the right and grasped it tightly for a second. Letting go, he said, "Not now. Compare my prints on both."

"The new fingerprints are considerably stronger and

clearer than the old."

"Surprise, surprise."

"It is not surprising because, as you know, the fatty substances that make up fingerprints evaporate slowly."

"But I've proved the point. My prints have hung around on this javelin for a year. How does their intensity compare with the ones on Crispy's arrow?"

"The amount of sebum is similar."

"Bob's your uncle!" Luke exclaimed. "The prints on the arrow are something like a year old, definitely more than a couple of days."

"Your analysis is not precise, so your deduction is doubtful. To make a valid comparison, the javelin and arrow would have to have been stored under identical conditions."

"I know. But answer this, Malc. With this evidence from the javelins, are my prints on the arrow more likely to be days old or months old?"

"They would appear to be months old."

Luke could not keep a triumphant grin from his face. "Thank you. Make sure that's in the case notes."

"Logged."

"Right. I want to see Rick Glenfield again." He made for the door of Ella's workshop.

"Rick Glenfield has finished his duties for the day and has just left the school premises."

Malc's announcement brought Luke to a halt. "By cab?"

"Confirmed."

Eagerly, Luke turned towards his mobile. "You're a nifty bit of kit, Malc. Where did he ask to be taken to?"

"A sports club in central Birmingham."

"Now why would he do that? He's got good sports stuff here. Perhaps he's been having archery lessons he didn't want the school to know about."

"Speculation."

"Yeah," Luke agreed. "But not for long. Tell me as soon as he gets back on site. I mean, immediately."

Chapter Twenty

"While we're waiting," Luke said to his mobile, "log on to the school computer again. I want to check the timing of something about four years ago. I hacked into the exam scores while Mr Glenfield was still an IT instructor. How long after that was he demoted to caretaker?"

It took Malc a few minutes to set up the link and locate the relevant files. "It was at the end of the same month."

Luke nodded. "Interesting. So my messing around was the final straw that got him demoted."

"That seems likely."

"You can't blame him for bearing me a grudge."

"I do not have the capacity to blame. . ."

"Yeah, but blame's big in Rick Glenfield's thinking," Luke said, talking to himself really. "If he reckons he gets blamed all the time – especially when something's not his fault – maybe he thinks he might as well commit the crimes. If he's going to take the rap for murder, he might as well do the killing."

"Spec..."

"I know," Luke said. "Speculation's the fun part that comes before a theory and proof. But think about it. He's got a motive for destroying me, he's got access to rattler venom and plenty of tools, and now he's off at a sports club where he could've polished up on his archery. On top of that, I reckon he had the chance to do all three killings. At least, he hasn't got alibis worth taking seriously. He's one of the few people who could stroll around the school in a nylon overall without looking shifty. That way, he could've protected his clothes from Vince's blood and hosed it down in Vince's shower afterwards. Then, just to make sure, he could've ripped it and binned it. And I still think he might've seen Crispy and Olivia together on the playing field, so he knew about them. Then, he's got all the computing skills to send Crispy a telescreen message that looked like it'd come from Olivia."

"Much of your reasoning is unproven."

"Yeah," Luke replied. "But he beats me to number one on the list."

Malc hesitated and then admitted, "Given recent findings, that is probably true."

"But, if he is Demon Archer, I still don't know why he'd use such a weird mixture of weapons."

A small crowd had gathered under floodlights to watch a game of baseball. If the murders hadn't happened, the contest would have drawn many more spectators. The sounds of their half-hearted cheers and groans, and the clunk of bat on ball, floated across the playing fields.

Having been told by Malc that Rick Glenfield had just used his identity card to re-enter the premises, Luke was strolling between the school gates and the main buildings, pretending that he needed some fresh air. Looking up, he noticed Rick Glenfield as if by coincidence and muttered, "Evening."

"Hello." Rick walked past him at pace.

"Oh," Luke called after him, trying to catch him off-guard. "Sorry, but I was going to ask you something else. What was it?"

With a sigh, Rick halted and turned towards him.

Acting, Luke lowered his head as if deep in thought and caught sight of Rick's holdall. "Looks like a sports bag," he commented. "Do you go to an outside club?"

Rick looked at him suspiciously but answered, "Yes." With the eerie glow of floodlights behind him, his face was shadowy and sinister.

"What for? The school's stuff is pretty good, isn't it?"

"Yes, but I don't like to use it. It's what I said about mixing with staff. It's not easy. I'm a fish out of water, remember. Besides, when I turn up at the gym here, they ask me to fix something rather than join in."

Luke nodded sympathetically. "Yes, I see the problem. No wonder you go somewhere else. Is it a good place?"

"It's all right."

"I might fancy going myself," Luke said. "You know,

to keep out of Ms Thacket's way. Has it got a swimming pool?"

"Yes, of course."

"Track?"

"Yes." Rick was getting uncomfortable, shuffling from foot to foot.

A cheer came from the pitch as one of the batters hit a home run.

"Archery?" Luke continued. "You know it used to be one of my things."

"Yes. They've got a practice range."

"Do you use it?" Luke glanced at his mobile as a way of reminding Glenfield that Malc could log on to the sports centre and find out.

"Sometimes." Trying to change the subject, Rick said, "What was it you wanted to ask me?"

"Oh, I know. Last sports day. You know, when I won the archery. Did you see anyone walk off with an arrow? Maybe a bow as well."

"That was a year ago."

"But did you see anyone?"

"Not that I remember."

"Okay. Here's an easier one. Not so long ago. This Tuesday, did Ms Kee bring those students to detention in the old kitchen herself?"

"No."

"But she must have known you were going to be there."

"Yes. We'd talked about it earlier in the day."

"Ah. Where did you talk?" Luke asked.

"Outside her office."

"Not in the place you're decorating?"

"No."

"Did you knock into her at all?"

Rick looked puzzled. "I don't think so." Then his expression changed and he added, "Thinking about it, she might have brushed against me when she came out. Is that what you mean? I'm pretty sure that happened."

Luke showed no reaction but he did not trust Glenfield's response. If the caretaker was guilty, he might have realized from Luke's line of enquiry that he'd left some particles on Ms Kee's clothing on Wednesday morning when he'd jabbed her with venom. Now, he could be trying to provide an innocent explanation. "Did you ever see Crispin Addley on our firing range – out of hours, I mean?"

"I told you I didn't really know him," Rick replied.

"Let me put it this way. Did you ever see a young couple meeting there?"

"I see a lot round the school – some things I'm not supposed to see, I guess – but no, not that."

Luke decided to apply more pressure. "I've been speaking to Olivia."

"Olivia?"

Luke's prime suspect did not fall into the trap of

knowing who she was. "The girl involved. She thought someone like you might have seen her with Crispin."

Rick shook his shaggy head. "Wasn't me."

"Just one more thing, then," Luke said. "Are you missing any tools at the moment?"

"Not that I'm aware of."

"Sure?"

"Are you after something in particular?"

"No. It doesn't matter." Turning away, Luke added, "Goodnight. And thanks."

On the pitch, the surly fielder standing at the third base of the diamond, Ed Hoffman, for once took his eye off the ball and watched Luke as he headed indoors.

Luke was stargazing sleepily from his bed. And thinking. "You know, there's no way of connecting Crispy with cat smuggling. I don't think that's got anything to do with it. It's about me, not endangered animals. Though, I guess, if someone's trying to have me put away or executed, that makes me endangered as well. Anyway, the cat's a red herring."

"Illogical and ridiculous."

Fighting against the weight of his eyelids to keep his eyes open, Luke said, "Is it? Why?"

Of course, Luke's joke was lost on Malc. "Because a cat lives in air and a herring in water. Besides, a herring is not. . . "

Luke interrupted. "Add to your programming, Malc. A red herring's a clue that leads us up the garden path."

"I cannot accept such a loose definition. You must be specific about which garden path."

Luke chuckled quietly. "Now, what made me think you'd say that? Add to your programming. Up the garden path means following a false lead."

"Entered."

"I've hardly stopped since Tuesday. I'm tired." Luke yawned and whispered, "Turn up the stars, Malc. I want it to look like a really clear night tonight. I want to drift off with them shining bright like diamonds."

As soon as he'd said it, Luke's spine tingled and he gasped. "That's it," he muttered to himself.

"Explain," Malc said.

Luke hesitated, savouring the moment. "No. I'll tell you in the morning. I'm going to sleep on it."

Under the false stars projected onto his bedroom ceiling, Luke slipped easily into a deep sleep with a wide smile on his face. At last, he understood the connection between the murder weapons.

Chapter Twenty-One

Luke never ran out of pomegranates. He never ran out of any food. Sensors in his smart kitchen kept track of his stocks and automatically sent out an order for more before he ran out of anything. The replacements were delivered by cab.

This morning, celebrating last night's success with the biggest pomegranate in his fruit bowl, Luke kept Malc waiting. His fingers dripping with blood-red juice, he said, "Do I detect impatience, Malc?"

The machine denied it. "I am not programmed to be either patient or impatient. However, I am aware of deadlines and sometimes remind you of them. You have a day and a half before your handling of the case is reviewed by The Authorities."

"Plenty of time, now I know what's going on."

"Explain."

Luke wiped his chin with a tissue that had already turned pink and soggy. "Yes, I will. After this. And a shower. I'm going to need one, it's so juicy."

Refreshed and looking forward to the day, Luke perched on the edge of his desk and picked up the arrow again. "The bit that does the damage, Malc. The point. What shape is it?"

"It is a parallelogram."

"Otherwise known as what?"

Malc answered, "A diamond."

Luke nodded. "Now Ms Kee. What killed her?"

"The venom of a rattlesnake."

"What snake precisely?"

"*Crotalus adamanteus*."

"And what's *adamanteus* in English? Put another way, what's the snake's common name?"

"It is the eastern diamondback rattlesnake. *Adamanteus* means like a diamond in hardness and lustre."

Luke nodded and smiled. "Are you getting the picture?"

"Confirmed. The cutting edge of a glass cutter is composed of very small diamonds."

"Exactly. Put this in your notes, Malc. Crispin Addley, Ms Kee and Vince Wainwright were all killed by diamonds of one sort or another. That's the connection. I know the staff call me Diamond so it's obvious Demon Archer's obsessed with framing me, presumably trying to wreck my career – and my life. So, let's narrow the suspects down, eh? As far as I know, Mr Cadman, Ella Fitch and Mr Bromley don't have anything against me, but some do bear me a grudge. Demon Archer knows my nickname. That'll include Rick Glenfield and Ms Thacket because they're staff.

I'm not so sure about students like Ed Hoffman and Shane." Luke paused for a few seconds, thinking, before he said, "Malc, search case notes for what Shane said to me on Tuesday. I want the bit that went, 'You're a pain,' or something like that."

Without any emotion, Malc recited, "You're a pain. Do you know that? Always have been. If our marks drop a bit, the instructors throw you at us every time. 'Luke Harding's marks didn't slip. Diamond performance.' Only Crispy had a chance of living up to it. And look what's happened to him." The sentences sounded dead without the passion that Shane put into them, as if they didn't mean anything.

Luke was nodding. One of the sentences meant a lot to him. "Diamond performance, eh?"

"Correct."

"So," Luke said, "it got to some students as well. Shane knows it. I don't know if Hoffman does."

"That may be irrelevant," Malc said.

"Irrelevant? Don't be daft. Why?"

"I have to point out that you could have committed all three killings with diamonds to live up to your nickname and reputation."

"What? You've got to be joking! That's what Demon Archer wants you to think. But I didn't even know they called me Diamond till Wednesday." He shook his head, dismissing Malc's theory. "With every new bit of evidence that comes in, I get less and less convinced that I did it. Even your electrons should see that. I bet Demon Archer didn't reckon on me being the FI in charge. He'd expect another investigator to be brought in, discover what the staff call me, see the diamond connection, and arrest me. Well, tough, because it hasn't worked out like that."

Malc had not yet come to the end of his objections. "It is not certain that someone who hates you enough to carry out such a bizarre plot actually exists. It seems more likely that any such person would simply murder you instead."

"Oh no, you're wrong. You've got to understand human nature. Killing me wouldn't do the job. No fun at all. Demon Archer wants to see me stripped of everything. If he – or she – did me in, everyone would feel sympathy for me. I'm supposed to go out in a blaze of disgrace, not drowning in sympathy. And Demon Archer probably wants to beat me on my home ground – using crime." Not allowing Malc time to reply, he got up and said, "Come on. I hope your batteries are up to speed. We've got a lot of work to do on nicknames and rattlers. You see, there are only two ways of getting rattlesnake venom. Milking a snake or getting someone else to milk it for you. So, the question is, why would anyone agree to supply somebody with a lethal venom? I've got an idea about that. It's back to the conservation park."

Only one of the two snake handlers at the animal sanctuary was available for interview. Luke was taken to a conference room to meet a keeper called Tim Izzard. The thirty year-old man was sitting stiffly, unnaturally, as if he were petrified to face a forensic investigator. He was trying too hard to keep calm – and keep his nerve – under difficult circumstances.

"Nothing to worry about," Luke began cheerfully. "I just wanted to ask you a few questions. Like, do you know Mr Cadman from the school?"

"Not well," Tim answered, "but he's been here a few times. He helps us out with some of the animals."

"Like eastern diamondback rattlesnakes?"

"Now you mention it, yes."

"Have you ever milked one for its venom?"

"Yes. Once. Ages ago – when Mr Cadman trained me. In case I ever had to do it again."

"And have you?"

"No," Tim replied.

"What about the other handler?" Luke asked.

Tim stiffened even more. For a moment, all he could do was utter her name, "Arlene."

Luke was puzzled by the man's reaction. "Yes, Arlene Dickinson."

"She's not in work," he said, keeping his face locked

into a neutral expression.

"Why not?"

Tim swallowed. "She. . . er. . . she died last night."

"What?"

"She died in front of a cab." Tim took a deep breath. "According to the coroner, there were no suspicious circumstances."

"She committed suicide."

Tim nodded.

"That's awful. I'm sorry. And I'm sorry I've got to bother you. But why did she do it? Do you know?"

Tim shrugged helplessly. "She's had something on her mind recently, depressed for a few days. Then she took a turn for the worse yesterday afternoon. But, no, I don't know why."

Feeling that Tim needed a break, Luke changed his approach. "What was Arlene like? Fond of animals, for sure."

"This was the only job she ever had. She loved it. Animals were her life, really. She cared about them – very deeply." Unable to sustain his rigid posture, Tim's head drooped at last.

"All animals? What about cats?"

Tim looked up again. "Especially cats. But we haven't had any snatched in the last few days. She wasn't feeling down because of that."

A different idea had formed in Luke's mind. It made

sense if the person who was trying to frame him for murder also knew that Ms Kee and Vince were dealing in stolen cats. Demon Archer could have met Arlene Dickinson and offered to eliminate the smuggling threat in return for some snake venom. If Arlene had agreed to the bargain, she might well have had second thoughts later and felt guilt-ridden about it. Already anxious about what had happened to the venom, somehow she could have heard about Ms Kee's murder yesterday afternoon and the responsibility might have been too much for her. It could have tipped her from depression into suicide. "Had she seen anyone from the school, just before this black mood?"

"Not that I know about."

"Did you see her talking to anyone unusual in the last few days?"

Tim shook his head.

"I'd like to have words with her partner," Luke said. "Who was she paired with?"

At once, Tim's face fell.

"Oh," Luke muttered. "I'm sorry. You're her partner."

"Yes," Tim answered.

"It must be very. . . "

"Yes. It's. . . regrettable."

He said it as if he were mourning the loss of a business partnership. Of course, in a way, that's what pairing was. It was about stability and control of the population. Love was not really part of the deal. And that's why Luke hated pairing.

While Luke struggled to think of something fitting to say, Tim continued, "I can't answer your questions. We weren't together every minute of the day so I don't know if she was in touch with the school or not. Like me, she knew Mr Cadman. That's all I know and unfortunately she's not here to tell you herself."

Luke was struck by the contrast between Olivia and Tim. When Crispy died, Olivia had failed to hold herself together. She had not even tried to turn up for lessons and sit stiffly, obediently, at a desk. And she shared everything with Crispy – except their future lives because they would never have been paired.

Trying to keep his mind on the job, Luke asked his final questions. "Could she milk a rattlesnake as well?"

Tim nodded. "Same training as me."

"Did she do it recently?"

"Not as far as I know, but I can't say she didn't."

"All right, Tim. This isn't a good time," Luke said. "I'll leave you in peace." Before he walked away from the troubled snake handler, he added, "But let me know if you think of anything or find something that tells you she was in touch with anybody else from the school. All right?"

"Yes, I will," Tim replied absently.

Chapter Twenty-Two

Back at school, Malc logged on to Mr Cadman's telephone record and confirmed that the science instructor had received several calls from the conservation park over a long period. The most recent entry was a conversation yesterday afternoon that lasted two minutes and thirty-four seconds.

"Not again!" Mr Cadman exclaimed when Luke and Malc turned up at morning break. The instructor grabbed his hat and slipped on his sunglasses.

"It won't take long," Luke said outside the staff room. "I just wondered if you knew someone called Arlene Dickinson at the conservation park."

"She's a very dedicated keeper."

"When did you last speak to her?"

"Face-to-face, some time ago. I can't remember. But she called me yesterday afternoon."

Mr Cadman was not showing any signs of knowing what had happened to Arlene after their conversation. Luke decided to get the information he wanted from the instructor before he let on. He didn't want Mr Cadman distracted by another death. "What was it about?" Luke asked.

"Well, it was supposed to be private."

Luke shook his head. "I don't think so. When there's a murder, we all lose our right to privacy. Solving the crime comes first."

Mr Cadman stared thoughtfully down the corridor for a few seconds and then said, "All right. I was considering catching up with you at lunch and telling you anyway. She wondered if there were any rumours going around about snake venom."

"Did you tell her about Ms Kee?"

Behind his sunglasses, he frowned. "Not in so many words. Not bluntly, but I guess I mentioned her memorial tomorrow."

"How would you describe Arlene's mood?"

Mr Cadman let out a sigh. "From her voice, I'd say she was upset."

"Did she say she'd been in contact with anyone at school – apart from you?"

"No."

"Sure?"

"Certain."

Luke felt that he had all he needed to explain Arlene's suicide, even though Malc would still regard his theory as unproven. He also had a duty to put Mr Cadman in the picture. Hesitantly, he said to the scientist, "I have to agree she was upset. Very upset. I'm afraid, after that call, she committed suicide."

Genuinely distressed, Mr Cadman muttered, "She

did what?"

"I don't think you should blame yourself." Luke knew what an FI should be doing. He should take advantage of Mr Cadman's state of shock and ply him with awkward questions. But Luke had not yet developed a hard heart. "I'm sorry to have to tell you, but you had to know." Instead of exploiting the situation, Luke asked only one more question. "You're obviously a clever man, Mr Cadman, so I think you know what this means. Does it change any of your answers?"

For once, he stripped off his sunglasses. "No. I'm just. . . appalled. Poor Arlene. And Tim." Replacing the shades again, he said quietly, "I guess you think she provided snake venom to someone in school. And you have me as her only contact. But I wouldn't need her help to get it, would I? I can't invent another contact just to save my skin. I don't know one. I just feel so sorry for her."

As Luke strode down the school corridors, Malc said, "I must intervene. You have considered Arlene Dickinson as the source of the venom that killed Ms Kee. This seems likely. However, would it have been sufficient reason for suicide? Her remorse would have been much greater if she had committed the murders rather than merely supplied a weapon. She should be a suspect."

"Maybe," Luke replied. "But not a serious one. First, she doesn't even know me, so I don't see how she could've had a grudge against me. If she wandered into the school at least three times, she'd have been spotted. From outside, she couldn't fake a telescreen message to Crispy. Most important, she didn't have a reason for killing him. He's not involved with cats or snakes or anything. The cat's a red herring, remember. If you want Arlene on the list," he said impatiently, "go ahead, but put her at the bottom. And, that reminds me, you can forget scanning everyone for cat hairs now."

"I assume you want me to stop performing the analysis rather than deleting the knowledge of it."

"Exactly."

Calling in on the sound studio, Luke found out that Jade didn't know he had a nickname amongst the staff. He got a very different response from Olivia Pang. Crispy's girlfriend was still cooped up in her quarters and, when Luke asked, she thought it was well known in her year that some of the instructors called him Diamond. "There's something else," Luke said to her. "Did you and Crispy know Ed Hoffman in my year?"

"No."

Turning to Malc, Luke said, "Plug yourself into the telescreen and give us his picture." When the photograph flashed up, Luke said, "Big guy. Not tall, I mean, but built big."

177

Olivia frowned. "Yes. I've seen him around. Into running and sport, isn't he?"

"Certainly is."

She looked embarrassed, but said nothing.

"What is it, Olivia?"

She glanced at Malc and remained silent.

"I'll keep you out of the case. I promise. But I really need whatever you're going to say on record this time. All right?"

Making up her mind, Olivia said, "I didn't know his name but he bumped into me and Crispy once – almost literally – on the field somewhere. He made a horrid remark to Crispy. I don't remember exactly what he said, but it was something about being as brainy as you and just as bad at picking girls."

"Thanks, Olivia," Luke said. "That's really helpful."

In the chaotic kitchen, Rick Glenfield did not attempt to hide the fact that he had been the one who had given Luke his nickname years ago. But he denied all knowledge of the people behind the cat smuggling.

"I want you to think back," Luke said to him. "When you were still in Information Technology, was Ms Thacket into computers?"

He shrugged. "I helped her out a few times with new software. She didn't take a particular interest as far as I remember, but she was good at getting to grips with all the stuff she needed."

Continuing his dash around the school, Luke caught Ms Thacket by the tennis and netball courts. The instructor took one look at him and grimaced. "I answered your questions on Tuesday."

"Yes," he replied as pleasantly as possible, "but I've got a few more now."

"I heard you were pestering people."

Ignoring her remark, he said, "I've seen you running over by the animal sanctuary. You must know it pretty well."

"I go round it, not in it."

Luke glanced down at her trainers and the bottoms of her tracksuit. He didn't need Malc to tell him that they were dotted with willowherb seeds. "Do you know any of the park staff?"

"No." She looked away from him and shouted at one of her netball players, "You're defence, Zara! What are you doing there? You've given possession away." She coughed twice and then turned sternly back to Luke.

"Where were you on Wednesday night, between ten-thirty and midnight?"

"What?" she exclaimed.

Calmly, Luke repeated the question that she'd already heard.

"I was with my partner. We were meeting friends in the city."

"Strange to be out enjoying yourself after Ms Kee's death."

"Look. It's grim in school right now. I needed a break."

"What time did you get back?"

"I don't know exactly. Why ask?" Ms Thacket pointed at his mobile. "That can check it to the nearest second."

Luke smiled. "Yes. That will." He knew Malc was just a machine but it still seemed rude to refer to him as if he were on a par with a smart fridge. He was a work colleague and as trusted as a friend.

Instructor Thacket cried out, "Yes, it must be very tempting to wallop Zara – I sympathise – but it's supposed to be a non-contact game."

Luke didn't know Zara in Year 7. He guessed that, with Ms Thacket on her back at every opportunity, she was more academic than sporty. Like Rick Glenfield, she looked like a fish out of water. It was plain that the flustered and breathless girl had joined the ranks of pupils resented by the sports instructor. Luke was wondering how far Ms Thacket had taken another one of her grudges – her grudge against him. "If you know what Malc can do, you must be used to computing."

"Only enough to do my job," she snapped.

"Did you see Ms Kee first thing Wednesday morning?"

"Yes."

"Where?"

"In her office before school."

"What for?" Luke asked.

"To fix a timetable problem."

"What sort of state was she in? Normal, agitated, ill? What?"

"She kept rubbing her forearm, grumbling she'd hurt it when someone bumped into her."

Luke nodded and outwardly remained cool. "Who was that?"

Ms Thacket shrugged. "No idea. She didn't say. I didn't ask. Why should I?"

"It doesn't really matter but did you see who it might have been? Was anyone hanging around near her office?"

"No. No one."

Hiding his disappointment, Luke changed the subject. "You must have heard the rumours about a trade in cats."

"Yes."

"What do you know about it?"

She shrugged. "It happens."

"Who's behind it?"

"Not just students, I heard."

"Which member of staff are you talking about?"

"I don't know, but has it happened since Wednesday?"

Luke smiled. "Are you suggesting Ms Kee?"

"You're the great investigator," Ms Thacket replied.

"It's not hard to work out."

"All right. On one of your runs around the field, did you ever see a couple getting together near the firing range after school?"

"That's not allowed."

Luke said, "No, but that's not the question. Did you ever see it?"

"No." She coughed loudly again.

"Getting a cold?"

"You're not interested in my sore throat."

To provoke her, Luke smiled again. "You don't like me so it must hurt to hear what the other staff call me."

"Diamond! I can think of a few diamond students and you're not one of them, Investigator Harding. You cheated with exam scores, you cheated at sports day and, as far as I know, you cheated everywhere else."

Luke didn't answer or defend himself. He had confirmed that Ms Thacket knew he was called Diamond. That was what he had come to check. It was also as clear as the snarl on her face that she still despised him. "Thanks," he said. "That's what I wanted to know. There's just one more thing, though."

"What?"

"Ed Hoffman. You're pretty close to him."

"So?"

"Did he know about Ms Kee and cats?"

"We mentioned it."

"You must have talked about me as well."

"Huh. You're not such a hot topic as you like to think. We've got better things to do with our breath."

"Like you, he'd be annoyed if he knew my nickname."

"Furious."

"So he does know?" Luke asked.

"Yes. Look. You were wrong to clash with him on sports day. Very wrong. You could have sent him out of control."

"Over a javelin?"

"It's nothing to do with a javelin and everything to do with loss of image. And the two of you clash because you're the same – rivals."

Luke was astounded. "The same?"

"Use your brain. That's what you're supposed to be good at. A top athlete like Ed doesn't come second. It's not an idea he can handle. It doesn't even cross his mind that second's nearly first. It's simply not good enough. More than that, it's complete failure. He'll do absolutely anything to come first and stay there. That's why Ed's a diamond athlete. You're supposed to be a diamond investigator. Can you imagine failing to catch your murderer? Can you imagine coming second? Of course you can't. You're the same as Ed." She looked away, scowling at Zara in one of her netball teams. Muttering, she added, "That's why you should've stuck with sport."

Chapter Twenty-Three

Luke held the tips of his forefinger and thumb one centimetre apart and said to Malc, "If Thacket was telling the truth, she came that close to seeing who jabbed Ms Kee."

"Unlikely," Malc replied. "She would have noticed such a close encounter and told you about it."

"All right. Let's agree she came within seconds or minutes of identifying Demon Archer."

"That is more probable."

"There's another explanation, of course," Luke added. "She might've bumped into Ms Kee herself and made up the bit about somebody else doing it. That would be a pretty convincing way of throwing suspicion at someone else."

"I have to warn you about bias. I detect that you are particularly keen to find evidence of her guilt."

Luke hesitated before replying. "Not true. I'm just doing my job. I'm particularly keen to find evidence proving anyone's guilt – apart from mine. By tomorrow. Interrogate the school computer again, Malc. What time did Instructor Thacket leave on Wednesday night?"

"Eight thirty-two."

"And what time did she get back?"

"The security record shows that she and her partner

used their identity cards to open the gates at eleven forty-four."

"She could've just made it to Vince's quarters, then. Maybe that's where she caught her cold – from Vince. On top of that, she found Crispy's body and she was perfectly placed to poison Ms Kee on Wednesday morning. They're facts, by the way, not bias. And now," he added, "it's lunchtime and I want the seat next to Shane."

Normally the canteen was a rowdy place. Since the murders, it had become relatively calm. Even so, Shane was sharing a quiet joke with a few friends on the next table. As soon as he spotted Luke, though, his face dropped and he adopted a more solemn manner.

Luke took his sandwiches to Shane's table and plonked himself down opposite the Year-10 student. "Phew," he said. "No matter how hard you think the instructors work you now, wait till you're in a job. It's non-stop."

Still wearing his blue denim jacket, Shane did not answer.

"Earlier," Luke continued in a quiet voice, "I saw a girl who's really down over Crispy. You don't seem to be in the same ballpark." He took a big bite out of his sandwich.

Immediately, Shane lost his temper. "That's a rotten

thing to say. It's awful about Crispy. I know it is. But he's gone. There's nothing I can do about that. Nothing anyone can do."

"You could help me find out what happened."

"What do you want to know now?"

"You're a member of the after-school animal club. You like rattlesnakes."

"So?"

"Do you know anything about their poison?"

Shane answered, "It kills people."

"Have you ever handled it?"

"The poison? Not likely."

Luke smiled and said to Malc, "That means no. It's not a statistical statement of the odds." Leaning towards Shane again, Luke asked, "Do you know what the staff call me?"

"A right pain, I should think."

"Apart from that."

Shane shrugged. "No idea."

"Are you sure?"

Shane looked fed up. "Certain."

Wondering why Shane was denying it, Luke said, "How about Diamond?"

"In your dreams. I've heard them talk about Luke Harding's diamond performance but that's different from being a good student. Look," he said, shuffling in his seat, "people like me have got to slave away for hours to get halfway to your marks. You just messed around but got the grades anyway. It's not fair. You were always in trouble with the instructors and The Authorities while the rest of us were cramming and still not coming up to scratch."

"I know I'm lucky," Luke replied. "But you sound really jealous."

Shane let out a grunt. "I wouldn't be in your shoes if you don't crack these murders soon. I'm not jealous of that."

Luke took a drink. He wasn't sure if Shane was so bent on revenge that he'd sacrifice Crispy – his best friend – to do it. Did Shane dislike him enough for that? "If you're in the animal club, you must know the animal sanctuary."

"Yes." Shane made his answer sound like a question.

"Do you know Tim Izzard and Arlene Dickinson, a couple of keepers?"

Shane shook his head. "I suppose I might recognize them if I saw them, but I don't know any of them by name."

"I want you to think really carefully. What did you do on Tuesday after Crispy went off to the playing field?"

"What do you mean?"

"I mean, did you follow him?"

"No!"

"What did you do, then?"

"I was working. On-line library work, if you must know."

Luke pointed at Shane's jacket and said, "There were blue denim fibres on Ms Kee's clothing. How do you explain that?"

Shane blushed but, after a few seconds, replied, "Why don't you ask everyone here, right now, to put their hands up if they're wearing denim?"

Unusually, Malc butted in. "I recommend you terminate this interview, FI Harding. You will want to review two new pieces of evidence as a matter of urgency."

Luke turned to Shane and said, "That's it for now. Got to dash." He left the remains of his lunch uneaten on the table.

Chapter Twenty-Four

The first was an archery bow that had been discovered in the school skip. Hurriedly pulling disposable gloves over his hands, Luke said with a big smile, "Let's not get excited. . ."

"I do not. . ."

"Well, I do. But not yet." Luke extracted the bow from the evidence bag and held it up by the string. "Over to you, Malc. I want the finest scan you've got. I want fingerprints and anything else. In fact, everything else."

When Malc had completed his examination, he reported, "The bow has been polished recently. It has no fingerprints whatsoever. I have identified twenty-four microscopic particles adhering to it but none appears to relate to the case. I suggest the bow was clean when it was placed in the skip with the rest of the rubbish. The traces that I have detected are almost certainly contamination by school waste."

Luke sighed and put the bow back in the bag. "Demon Archer knows how to shoot straight and how to wind up a forensic investigator."

The second new piece of evidence to be found in the skip was smaller but even more significant to the case. It was a fragment of light green cotton, about the same size as Luke's palm. It was charred around its edge because someone had attempted to destroy the garment by burning it. The ploy had nearly worked. In a pile of ash, it was the only material to survive the fire. And it had two small red stains.

Again, Luke's heart drummed faster and louder. "Let's take it a step at a time. Just confirm these stains are blood, not pomegranate juice, Malc. Then do a full comparison with Vince's." He laid out the cloth on a clean piece of polythene on his desk.

While Malc hovered above the cotton fragment, examining both stains, Luke sat back and chewed a fingernail. His mobile was a state-of-the-art analytical instrument, capable of completing many tests amazingly quickly but, at times like this, never quickly enough.

Malc did not have to struggle to locate the stains this time. "Positive reaction to the oxidation of luminol, confirming the presence of haemoglobin. It is blood." There was another delay before Malc's next announcement. "Fluorescent antibody analysis confirms that it is human blood."

Luke waited in silence for the results of the protein electrophoresis and DNA fingerprinting. The only sounds he could hear were Malc's gentle whirring and his own heart thudding even more rapidly.

"It has the same blood group as Vince Wainwright."

Luke nodded. One test – the most important one – to go. And it would be the longest wait. The minutes seemed to stretch into hours.

"The DNA profile is identical to the blood in Vince Wainwright's bathroom."

"Bob's your uncle!" Luke cried. "It's what Demon Archer was wearing on Wednesday night. A lucky break, at last."

"Incorrect," Malc replied. "You underestimate yourself. You requested a search of the waste. Luck did not play a part."

"No, I mean, lucky that a bit of it survived." With tweezers, he turned it over to find that his luck was holding. Part of a label was intact: '*Men's Fas-*'. At once, Luke said, "Malc. Get on to Men's Fashion Incorporated right now and send them details of this cloth. It looks like it's from the neck of a shirt. I want anything on its distribution and sales. And I want it pronto. I wish I could read its size but. . ." He shrugged. "Still, I've already taken a big step forward. You know what I mean, don't you?"

"It is the first evidence that Demon Archer is a man."

"Exactly. I've never seen Ms Thacket in a man's shirt. Come to think of it, I've never seen her in anything but sports gear. Anyway, she's out of the picture." Luke nodded towards the inside surface of the cloth. "Microscopic scan, Malc. Find me some skin or a hair from Demon Archer and I'll have him through his DNA."

Twenty seconds later, Luke's run of good fortune came to an end. "The only particles on this side are carbon."

Luke let out the breath he'd been holding. "You mean soot. The fire charred any trace of the man wearing it."

"Correct."

Luke shook his head. "Pity." Carefully, he put the material back into its evidence bag. Trying not to be too disappointed, he said, "Ms Thacket nearly saw him on Wednesday morning. Now I've got part of something he was wearing when he killed Vince." He brought his forefinger and thumb together again. "This time, I was that close. I'm homing in, Malc." Switching back to the routine investigation, Luke added, "For now, though, there's something left over from my chat with Shane. Link to the on-line library and check his usage on Tuesday after school."

"He logged on to the system at four nineteen and logged off at five thirty-seven."

"Okay. Can you monitor his activity in between?"

"No."

"So, his computer might not have been doing anything. He could've logged on, gone out, and come back later to log off, thinking he'd got himself an alibi."

"I cannot discount that possibility."

"Okay. But right now I want to concentrate on a more likely suspect. What I need is a clean piece of paper, a comb and Rick Glenfield."

"Sit down," Luke said to the startled caretaker, waving him towards the chair on the other side of the desk.

Rick looked nervous and uncomfortable in Luke's quarters. Eyeing the clean white paper that covered the table top, Rick asked, "What's it about this time?"

"I see you've got your new overall," Luke remarked.

"What do you want from me?"

"Do you think I lost you your job?"

"No. Well, partly, yes," he replied. "I don't know what would have happened if you hadn't broken into the exam system. I would've hung on longer, that's for sure."

"I'm sorry about that – really sorry – and I'm sorry I've got to get you to do something for me now but. . ." He shrugged. "Do you have a comb?"

Bewildered, Rick answered, "A comb? Yes."

"Right. I want you to bend your head over the table and comb your hair – and beard – very thoroughly so anything that comes out goes onto the paper."

"You what?"

Luke said, "Sorry but you don't have a choice."

"You can't. . ."

"Malc. Am I within my rights to ask for this?"

"You are following legal procedure."

The ginger teddy bear looked devastated, as if his dignity was taking yet another pounding. Even so, he got his comb out of his trouser pocket and mechanically began to run it through his mass of hair.

"More on the right, please," Luke said, feeling pity for the caretaker. "And the beard."

Rick's face was bright red. He glanced at Luke in disgust but carried on with the humiliating exercise.

Eventually, Luke said, "That's fine. Thanks. And sorry again to put you through that but it's necessary, believe me. Now," he added, "we move away and let Malc do his job."

The mobile did not take long to scan the table top. "Nine hairs, three small pieces of vegetable matter, many fragments of dead skin, three particles of soot and one of ash."

"Ash and soot," Luke repeated. "How do you explain that?"

Rick shook his head. "I don't know."

"In that case, I've got to ask you to surrender your identity card to the school secretary. He will downgrade it so it can't be used outside the school. I'm confining you to the premises."

"But. . ." Rick's objection died on his lips. He mumbled to himself, "That's right. Blame me. Again."

"That's all for now," Luke said. "You can go."

"Not far, I can't."

Before the downcast caretaker could reach the door, Luke called after him, "By the way. Your sports centre.

Does it do weightlifting?"

Rick sighed. "Yes."

"Do you?"

"Yes. A bit."

"That's good. Thanks."

As soon as Rick Glenfield left, Luke said to Malc, "I'll bag up this stuff from Rick's hair but then we're off to the gym. My brain needs a workout. Those specks of soot got me thinking about all the other trace evidence. The one I've been neglecting is the magnesium carbonate – magnesite – on Ms Kee. You said it's used to make non-slip concrete flooring. I bet it's not just floors."

Mr Bromley was overseeing the last lesson of the week in the gym. In the main arena, a game of basketball was under way. To the left, there was a small cluster of students around the bars and weights. Two were queuing to use the chalk that would provide them with extra grip. Every time someone dipped hands into the tub, a small white cloud bloomed.

"Go over, Malc, and test the chalk. To a scientist, chalk's calcium carbonate but I bet that's not."

Being a metal machine, Malc could not smile. Having a neutral synthetic voice, he could not sound satisfied. But, before he gave his verdict, Luke could tell from his mobile's manner that he had returned with an

interesting result.

"The weightlifting chalk is finely ground magnesite."

Luke grinned and nodded with satisfaction. "Magnesium carbonate for non-slip floors and non-slip hands. And it's so fine it'll get everywhere. Even after washing hands I bet some's left under the fingernails." He paused before adding, "Ms Kee was no bodybuilder so she picked the magnesium carbonate up from someone who is. If it was under Demon Archer's nails when he bumped into her and jabbed her, a bit could've got on her clothes. Which leaves us with two suspects way out in front."

"Explain."

"Glenfield and Hoffman. I'm not counting Shane. Have you got a record of him weightlifting?"

"No."

"No. He's not exactly bulging with muscles. It's down to Rick Glenfield or Ed Hoffman." Luke paused for thought and then said, "I reckon both have been sharpening up their archery skills on the quiet. And what does Hoffman's file say about his computer skills?"

"Until he opted for sport, he showed some promise."

"So, he could play tricks with a telescreen message to Crispy?"

"Not known, but it is a possibility."

Malc fell silent for a moment and then he said, "I have just received a message. Men's Fashion Inc to

Investigator L Harding. The green cotton is from a man's shirt. It is made in all sizes from junior to extra-large. It has been sold nationwide, including Birmingham, for the last ten months and continues to be a midrange market leader. When it first came out, market research suggested it was fashionable among middle-aged women but that trend has now lapsed. End of message."

"Mmm. That doesn't exactly narrow it down, does it?"

"It does the opposite. I suggest you make Ms Thacket a major suspect again."

Chapter Twenty-Five

When Luke asked Ed Hoffman to press down on the skin of his fingertips to reveal what was lurking behind his fingernails, the student's expression was murderous. "You want me to do what?" There was spite and resentment in his wild eyes.

"Hold up your hands so my mobile can scan what's under your fingernails," Luke replied.

"You're pushing your luck, Harding." Reluctantly, Ed did as he was told.

Almost immediately, Malc reported, "There are several deposits of fine magnesium carbonate."

"What's that mean?" Ed snapped.

"Not a lot," Luke answered. "It means you're a weightlifter, that's all."

"Well, congratulations on your amazing detective work! You've made a real breakthrough."

"There are also four specks of carbon on the shoes," Malc added after completing a body scan.

"Soot, eh. That's more unusual for a weightlifter," said Luke. "How come?"

"Don't get excited. That's easy as well. I burnt some toast this morning. I scraped the black stuff off. I guess some fell on my shoes. It doesn't mean I'm into arson if that's what you're getting at."

To Luke, Ed's answer seemed unforced. It was either true or well prepared. "You've never handled cats. I know because you told me."

"That's right."

"But do you know who was handling them?"

"No."

"Have you been over to the conservation park?"

"What for? Why should I?"

"No idea," Luke replied with a shrug. "But have you?"

"No."

Just before Luke walked away, he said, "Oh, you know that last detention you did for Ms Kee? Well, I just want to get it clear in my mind. You sanded a white table top down to the wood and then polished it with wax. Right?"

"More great detective work."

"Is that right? You used wax polish?"

"Yeah."

"Thank you," Luke said.

It was Friday evening and, in his quarters, Luke was feeling downbeat. This morning, he'd been confident that he would have solved it by now. But he hadn't. Not really. Thinking through all of the evidence, he still had three clear suspects. Rick Glenfield came closest to filling Demon Archer's shoes, but the battered caretaker was not Luke's first choice. Life had been cruel to

Glenfield and it showed no sign of letting up. If Luke had tried to explain his reasoning to Malc, though, his mobile would have ripped his argument to pieces. Rick's bad luck and Luke's gut feelings meant nothing to the law.

In his mind, Luke replayed his final qualification exam. There'd been a point near the end of the test when he thought he'd cracked the problem but actually he'd got more than one solution. Then, evidence of high-jumping had come to his rescue. This time, when it was a real case, weightlifters' chalk had not turned into a trump card. Ms Thacket, Ed Hoffman and Rick Glenfield all used it. Even the cotton from the burnt shirt had let him down. What he needed – and what would persuade Malc – was a syringe with Demon Archer's fingerprints on the barrel and Ms Kee's blood on the needle. But it hadn't turned up.

Tomorrow, The Authorities would assess Luke's progress and, almost certainly, strip him of the case.

Interrupting Luke's gloomy thoughts, Malc said, "I have received a computer message from Rick Glenfield. He claims that he collected rubbish from the various bins around the school yesterday and dumped it into the skip, ready for collection. He is wondering if that is the origin of the ash and soot in his hair."

Luke smiled wryly because he knew that the statement wasn't reliable. It would not help Rick's cause. "How long did it take him to come up with that explanation?"

Unable to recognize that Luke did not expect an answer, Malc replied, "Five hours and seven minutes."

"Mmm. It might be true, of course, but anyone could come up with something pretty convincing with five hours to think about it." The message was not the clincher that Luke was hoping for. He closed his eyes and took three deep breaths. Then, perking up, he got to his feet and said, "I'm going to see Jade."

At once, Malc began to hover, ready to accompany him.

"No, Malc. On my own."

"I recommend. . . "

"I don't think it's a good idea for you to come as well."

"Explain."

"Because you might not approve of what I've got in mind."

"If it affects the case, I must be present."

"What do you want, Malc? I think I can crack it tomorrow morning if you keep out of it, or do you want to be in on the idea and stop me because it's. . . unconventional."

"You have a habit of using words loosely. Do you mean illegal?"

"Ms Thacket was right. I'll do anything to solve a

case. But I promise you, it's not really illegal. Honest, Malc. It's just that the law wouldn't approve. It's not official procedure. If you really want to see me finish this one off, you'll stay here so you don't hear anything you'd be forced to send to The Authorities."

Malc was silent for a few seconds and then said, "My power level is less than optimum. I will remain here to recharge."

On his way out, Luke said, "Thanks, Malc. And nicely put, by the way." He hesitated in the doorway, his expression more cheerful than it had been all evening. "That's the thing with you, isn't it? You never lie."

"The programming of every mobile aid to law and crime allows only the truth. It is a central principle of the law. Without it, trust in the system breaks down."

Luke nodded. "Perfect," he muttered before he disappeared towards Jade's quarters.

Jade's hand shot to her cheek. "Hiya," she said as cheerfully as ever. But her bloodshot eyes told a different story.

"Are you all right?" asked Luke.

"Fine. Great, actually. I've just. . . I'll tell you later."

"Tell me what?"

"Later."

"Tell me now."

"No," she said. "I can't."

"If you can tell me later, you can tell me now. Come on. Spit it out."

"All right, all right." She took a deep breath. "I've just got my first posting. It's brilliant. I'm very happy. You ought to see the equipment they're going to give me. They said they want me – me – to be the future of music, Luke." She paused before adding, "I'm going to Sheffield."

Luke needed all of his strength to celebrate with her. "That's fantastic. Sheffield's the place to be for music. Excellent. I'm really pleased." But he couldn't keep it up. His control deserted him and he let out a tiny tell-tale moan. "When do you go?"

"Next weekend."

"Next weekend?"

She nodded.

"So, we've only got a week."

With eyes bright and moist, she said, "That's right."

Luke hugged her and whispered, "Congratulations."

"They said I'm going to be really big in music. Like you in law."

"I bet they're interested in your spotlight sound."

"Very."

"Me too."

Jade pulled away from him a little. "What do you mean?"

It was difficult for Luke to drag himself back to the

case when Jade had just announced their separation. But he needed his job to distract him from the coming loss. It was too painful to think about. He said, "I'd like you to help me with something."

"Anything," Jade replied.

"You're doing the music for Ms Kee's memorial tomorrow, aren't you?"

Jade nodded. "From the balcony."

"Perfect. If you record a few words from me now, you can distort them, can't you?"

"Yes. But how do you mean?"

"I mean, make my voice sound flat and neutral. Synthetic really."

"Like Malc's, you mean?"

"Exactly."

Chapter Twenty-Six

Everybody was required to attend the ceremony. Filled with the overpowering scent of lilies, the Great Hall was seething with students and staff. In the traditional manner for a memorial, the younger pupils were sitting in straight lines in front of the stage. The older students, from Year 6, were standing. Furthest back were the ones who, like Luke and Georgia, had graduated but not yet left the school. The instructors and other staff were standing solemnly around the outside. The only sounds were the speakers' tributes and an occasional suppressed cough. Spotlights were trained on the flower-strewn stage and the hall itself was dimly lit.

The speeches were not that long – together they lasted an hour – but to an edgy Luke they seemed endless. From his position near the back of the hall, he glanced upwards but all he could see was the base of the overhanging balcony. He couldn't see Jade above him but he was comforted to know that she was there. He glanced sideways and caught sight of Ms Thacket, her head bowed. Luke suspected that she was hiding her face in case it revealed a lack of grief. In front of him was the unmistakable figure of Ed Hoffman. When Luke looked the other way – to his right – Georgia gave him a faint smile. Beyond her, at the far side, Rick Glenfield was staring into the distance, listening to the tributes. The caretaker's expression suggested bewilderment and near panic. In the corner, Ella Fitch was standing with a remote control in her hand. Behind Luke, Malc hovered like a faithful friend.

Within the next hour, Luke would arrest Demon Archer or, if he was wrong and his prime suspect was innocent, he would be disgraced. He took a deep breath, trying to keep his nerves at bay.

Eventually, the final speech brought the formal part of the service to an end. Ella pressed a key on her remote control and the level of general lighting increased. The staff and students were then free to break ranks but the ceremony continued. Everyone was invited to share drinks and fond memories of Ms Kee in small groups. It was considered disrespectful to refuse either, so no one left. The Great Hall was awash with whispers, mostly praising Ms Kee's dedication to the school and her relentless pursuit of discipline.

They would not be the only whispers. From the balcony, Jade Vernon was providing the perfect atmosphere with music – not too loud, not too soft, not too morbid, not too merry. She was also making the final adjustments to a probe that looked like the barrel of a gun.

Underneath the balcony, Georgia made for Luke. "How's it going?" she asked. "You were asking about cats and rattlers."

Georgia could hardly have picked a worse time. He needed to concentrate on his plan. He had to get near to Ed Hoffman in a position that Jade could see. "It's. . . fine. Thanks. I'm sorry, Georgia, but I've got to. . . "

She put her hand on his forearm. "Did you hear Ms Kee's pairing plans before she. . . you know?"

The easiest option was to pretend that he didn't know that they had been chosen to be partners and move away, but Georgia did not deserve deceit. "Yes," he answered. Struggling for the words, he said, "You know, anyone would think they're really lucky to be paired with you, Georgia. Me included. But. . . " He hesitated and sighed. "Look, I. . . "

"It's okay. I know about you and Jade. I understand."

"Oh?"

"Friendship and pairing are two different things, aren't they? You can still be friends with her."

"But Jade and me, we're. . . "

"The two of you are close, but worlds apart, Luke. Sorry, but that's the way it is. The only thing I don't know is if anything's changed because of Ms Kee."

Malc interrupted. "When I searched all of the deputy head's files, I discovered that the latest batch of pairings were provisional. Yours has not been authorized by the Pairing Committee. Once a new Chair has been appointed, the pairings will be reviewed and approved."

Georgia paused for a moment and then said to Luke, "Well, I guess we have to wait and see. But I just wanted you to know I'm pleased." With a smile, she turned and walked away.

For a moment, Luke didn't move. He watched her retreat and felt sad that the Pairing Committee would almost certainly put her in an awful position – somewhere between him and Jade. That would be Ms Kee's legacy. He also felt guilty that he'd be forced to hurt her feelings because he could not let go of Jade.

Luke manoeuvred his way through the gathering until he was somewhere near the centre of the Great Hall. Looking up over his shoulder, he spotted Jade leaning on the rail of the balcony, looking down at him. He gave a slight nod of acknowledgement. In return, Jade pointed left, telling him where he needed to go.

Following her guidance, he collided with Ella Fitch almost at once.

"Good, isn't she?" the technician said.

"What? Who?" Luke asked.

Ella nodded in the direction of the balcony. "Your friend. She creates a good atmosphere."

"Oh, yes. Better than good."

Ella came very close to him and whispered, "Be careful, Diamond. Just because Ms Kee's not with us any more doesn't mean you and Jade Vernon. . . There's plenty more like Ms Kee in The Authorities. You can't sabotage every javelin that life throws at you."

"Yes. I know. Thanks."

Using his considerable height to locate Ed Hoffman and Ms Thacket, Luke carried on edging towards them. When he was only a couple of paces away, he stopped and found himself next to Mr Cadman. The science instructor was not wearing his sunglasses and hat. Luke guessed that it was a sign of respect for Ms Kee.

"I ought to come clean about something you pupils never knew," Mr Cadman said. "You only thought of Ms Kee as someone who handed out punishments but, behind the scenes, she was very supportive of science and criminology. She was also very proud of many students – particularly the troublesome ones who came good in the end." He gazed significantly at Luke and then looked around to check that he would not be overheard. Lowering his voice, he said, "Have you learnt any more about poor Arlene? And who she gave snake venom to – if that's what happened?"

Deliberately, Luke did not keep quiet. "I'm very confident I know what happened."

With his back towards Luke, Ed Hoffman glanced over his shoulder and sneered.

"And?" Mr Cadman prompted.

"And what?" said Luke.

"What's the story?"

Luke smiled. "You won't have long to wait." He took

a quick look at Jade and nodded again.

Jade had three short recordings of sampled voices. The first was her own and the other two belonged to Luke but they did not sound like him. She had modified them to sound like a machine.

Down below her, Luke was talking to Mr Cadman but he had also got himself into a position near Ed Hoffman. She squatted so she could line up her spotlight transmitter precisely. Luckily, Ed was standing still as he talked with Ms Thacket. Jade adjusted the probe so that her recorded voice would be focused on his right ear. The first transmission would be a trial to check that he could hear her words. They were words that Luke had chosen to unsettle and annoy Ed.

Convinced that she'd got it lined up, she flicked a switch to send out the tight beam of sound. "Brilliant, Luke! You're a diamond investigator."

At once, Ed turned round and, looking puzzled, glared with hatred at Luke.

Ed's reaction meant that Jade's sound system was working beautifully. He had heard the voice in his ear, like a whisper. No one else reacted so she knew that the sound had hit the right spot. It had flown past everyone else in total silence.

Jade aligned the probe again in case Ed had moved his position. This time, Hoffman would hear a flat voice like

Malc's. With luck, he'd think it was Malc's. And knowing that a Mobile Aid to Law and Crime never lies, he'd believe every word. She waited for the next signal from Luke and then let loose the ghostly message.

"I have just received the results on the syringe. It has both Ed Hoffman's fingerprints and Ms Kee's blood on it."

From the balcony, Jade watched Ed spin round in horror. He stared at Luke and then at Malc. When neither of them made a move towards him, he turned away again. For the brief moment that she could see his expression full on, she glimpsed surprise but not denial. The blush on his face was probably nothing to do with embarrassment and everything to do with anger, possibly even madness. In that instant, Jade knew that Luke was right. Ed Hoffman had murdered three people.

She knelt down, ready to fire the final recording.

The trick was working. Jade's aim was spot on. Luke heard Ms Thacket say, "Are you all right, Ed?"

In shock, Ed muttered, "Yes."

Yet his manner told everyone nearby that he was slowly crumbling under a pressure that they didn't understand.

Luke glanced up towards Jade. That would be enough to get her to beam down the last message that would be inaudible to everyone else in the vicinity.

Luke tensed, wondering how Ed would respond when he thought that he heard Malc say, "I confirm there is now sufficient evidence to charge Ed Hoffman with murder."

Five seconds later, Luke got an answer.

Ed swung round again. This time, there was a knife in his hand.

Chapter Twenty-Seven

There was an audible gasp from everyone who could see what was happening. Right away, they drew back and left a small arena in which Luke faced the formidable figure of Ed Hoffman.

Luke stood like a statue, unable to move. The only part of him that was still working was his brain. "Don't do it, Ed. Look, you've got lots of witnesses and Malc in record mode. You can't get away with it." He tried to sound normal but his voice quaked.

Ed was smirking as he prowled around the ring of people, not yet closing in on his prey.

A drop of sweat ran down Luke's left cheek. While talking to Ed yesterday afternoon, Luke had convinced himself that he'd discovered the identity of Demon Archer. Two of Ed's answers just hadn't added up. But Luke didn't have quite enough evidence to convince the law, so now he had to extract a confession in front of witnesses. It was very dangerous because he needed to provoke Ed even more.

Luke said, "People who go running round the animal sanctuary get willowherb seeds on their trainers. But you got them on your ordinary shoes. You don't run in them. You were lying when you said you didn't go to the park. You met Arlene."

"Trying to be clever in front of an audience again, Diamond?"

"Arlene gave you the snake venom in return for stopping the trade in cats. You told me you didn't know who was involved, but Ms Thacket did and she talked to you about it. So, that's another lie." Luke was praying that he was right. He had written off Ms Thacket as a suspect because she would not have admitted that she knew who was smuggling cats if she had been Arlene's contact. Fixing his eyes on Hoffman, Luke said, "And there was that wood polish and sawdust in detention. You got a bit of the wax on Ms Kee when you bumped into her on Wednesday, and you left some sawdust in Vince's quarters."

Ed had completed an entire circle around Luke, like a stalking animal. All the while, he was creeping closer as if he intended to spiral in before taking his victim.

Seeing the vicious knife in Ed's hand, no one else dared to move.

Luke knew that Malc would have already put out an emergency call for assistance but the guards would be minutes away. Before they arrived, Luke needed to build a rock-solid case against Ed. So far, he had remained tight-lipped. Somehow, Luke had to taunt him into revealing his guilt. After all, Ed had nothing to lose any more because he thought the case against him was foolproof and he was about to be charged. Luke had only to catch him out and then stay alive until help arrived.

"How did you find out about Vince Wainwright? Did you see him coming back with cats one time when you were on a run? I bet you did."

Still no response.

"What about the soot on your shoes?" Luke continued. "Nothing to do with overdone toast. You tried to burn your green shirt, Ed. The one you wore when you killed Vince. But it didn't work. There was a bit left. I've got it."

"You make me sick."

"It's a funny weapon you used to kill him." Luke shrugged, pretending to be baffled. Giving Ed an opportunity to prove himself superior, he asked, "Why?"

"Don't you know anything?" Ed snarled.

"I thought so, but you've got me beat with that one."

"Huh. You're no diamond if you don't know glass cutters have got diamond edges."

That sentence justified Luke's tactics. It was the statement that would condemn Hoffman because no one but the murderer and Luke knew how Vince had been killed. Yet Luke could not feel relief while Ed still waved the blade back and forth menacingly. In his quivering voice, Luke asked, "Why did you kill them, Ed?"

"You know why."

"Tell me."

Ed came nearer and nearer, still grasping the knife in his hefty fist. "I hate you. You cheated with that javelin. You cheat over everything. You made me look a fool."

"But you killed three people – because you hate me!"

"They were nothing. Just pawns."

"You should've killed me."

Ed laughed. "Not good enough. I wanted you to suffer. I wanted to see you ruined. An investigator sent down for murder!" He paused and then continued his prowl. "But it's all changed now. You can have your wish. If I can't get you convicted, I'll sentence you myself. A diamond cheat deserves the death penalty. You know that's what I'm going to do, don't you?"

The people gathered around gasped again but did not dare to intervene. Further back, staff and students strained their necks to see what was happening.

"No, you won't," Luke replied. "Everyone's watching." Now, he could feel the sweat running down his back and soaking into his shirt. His heart was beating at twice its normal rate and his stomach was churning so much, he thought that he was about to vomit.

"You're not that smart. Think about it, Harding. You've got me for three murders. One more won't make any difference."

Abruptly, Ed took a step closer and aimed the first blow down at Luke's chest.

Startled, Luke could not react quickly enough to save himself from the blade.

But the stabbing pain and the warm blood never came.

Malc darted between the boys at amazing speed. The blow landed on his metallic shell and sent him crashing to the floor and skidding into the crowd. The weapon went in the opposite direction.

Most of the onlookers were so stunned by the spectacle and so scared of Ed Hoffman that they didn't budge. A few people would have tried to help but each of them waited for someone else with the courage to make the first move.

Ed himself was the first to react. His fist thudded into Luke's stomach, then he sprang after the knife. He snatched it up and, in a flash, he was standing over Luke.

Nauseous and totally winded, Luke had doubled up in agony.

Ed looked around briefly, a warped smile on his lips in his moment of triumph. In his madness, he seemed pleased to be performing to an audience again. He had lost the javelin competition in front of the whole school – he had lost face in front of the whole school – and now it was clear that he was making up for the humiliation with the same spectators. Taking a deep breath, he stretched out both arms, preparing to plunge the blade down into the back of Luke's neck.

But he froze.

For a split second, Ed hesitated. Then he dropped the knife, clamped his hands to his ears and screamed.

Everyone who had watched him in the javelin competition had been surprised by his unexpected performance. This time, they were utterly amazed. They were mystified because they couldn't hear anything but Ed's cry of pain.

An intolerably loud noise was bombarding Ed and Ed alone.

Wheezing, Luke took a deep breath. Clutching his stomach, he kicked away the knife and dragged himself upright. Malc came unsteadily out of the crowd just in time to record Luke's arrest. "Ed Hoffman. I have sufficient evidence to charge you with the murder of Vince Wainwright, Crispin Addley and Ms Kee."

Malc added, "And the attempted murder of Forensic Investigator Luke Harding."

It was unlikely that Ed heard anything. He collapsed to the floor.

Jade rushed down the steps and threw herself against the door at the back of the hall. Bursting through, she cried, "Luke!"

Still spellbound, everyone looked round. When the people nearest to her saw that she was charging towards the centre, they shuffled aside.

Shouldering a way through the channel, she burst into the middle and made for Luke who was still struggling for breath. "Are you all right?" she almost shouted in her anxiety.

Trying to ignore his tender midriff, he muttered, "I'm fine." He took another breath and said, "Thanks, Jade. Brilliant idea. I owe you."

Forgetting everyone else, Jade grabbed his arm in both her hands to help him stand up straight. Glancing at Hoffman, beginning to stir on the floor but still holding his head in his hands, she said, "I cranked the music up to ear-splitting and fed it through the spotlight probe. He would've thought his brain was about to burst."

Managing a grin, Luke complained, "You took your time, though."

"No pleasing some people," she retorted. "Under the circumstances, I set it up pretty quickly. But he kept moving. I couldn't focus on him."

Georgia had also edged her way to the centre of the action. Seeing Luke in Jade's arms, she flushed deep red.

There was a disturbance at the front of the Great Hall and the crowd parted again. This time, guards were coming to take Ed Hoffman away.

Chapter Twenty-Eight

"Why did you do it, Malc?"

"What are you referring to?"

Luke and Malc were going through every item of evidence, making sure that each one was correctly labelled for use as an exhibit in Ed Hoffman's trial. "If you hadn't come between me and Hoffman, I wouldn't be here now. Which bit of your programming told you to do that?"

"My first duty is to the law. I did it to prevent a crime. Also, it was logical to keep you alive to conclude the case."

"Oh, yeah." Luke grinned. "If Hoffman had attacked Jade, I'd have been in there like a shot. Nothing to do with the law, everything to do with affection. You didn't do it because you like me, did you?"

"I do not have the capacity for affection."

"Are you sure?"

"Confirmed."

Luke laughed. "I'm pulling your leg."

"I do not possess a leg."

"Come on. Admit it. Isn't there a circuit somewhere that's pleased with itself?"

"Negative."

"Hey. I thought you'd agreed to say no instead of

negative. You're not trying to get your own back by annoying me, are you?"

"Negative."

"Mmm." Luke looked at Malc suspiciously. "Anyway, I reckon we might make a pretty good team yet."

It was the last night that Luke and Jade would be together and they'd decided to spend it in the open air. Without Malc. They were lying down on the firing range, but keeping well clear of the spot that was marked with a sad and ragged bunch of lilies. That was where Luke's first case had begun with an arrow and Crispin Addley.

It wasn't particularly cold but, for comfort, they huddled under a blanket. The sky was beautifully clear, reminding Luke of another night he'd spent outside a long time ago, wrapped in a thick blanket. To the north, where particles from the sun were crashing into the upper atmosphere, a superb swirl of ghostly green shimmered. Earlier in the day, the weather forecasters had predicted that, after tonight, the rain would finally arrive and cloud would obscure the glittering stars.

Luke was quiet and thoughtful for lots of different reasons. Eventually, he sighed and whispered, "Of course, Ed would say I cheated again."

"You just used a bit of imagination and creativity. Like a real artist," Jade replied. "And you solved it. Mission accomplished. Time to look forward."

The night was gorgeous and so was Jade. She'd become a redhead again. But Luke didn't really want to look forward. Far from welcoming a new day, he wanted time to stall. He wanted to share this night with her for ever. Tomorrow, Jade would leave for Sheffield. A few days afterwards, he'd be sent south.

With her eyes on the heavens, Jade said, "This was a lovely idea, Luke. It feels naughty, silly and romantic all at the same time."

"I stayed outdoors overnight once before. I was. . . I don't know. Too young to remember – less than five. But, like this, it was beautiful and sad as well."

"Sad?"

"I'm sure it was. I think it was some sort of parting."

"Like tomorrow," Jade said, her voice breaking.

"I don't know. Maybe. But something tells me it wasn't quite the same."

Waving mechanical arms, ten moonlit giants watched over them from the edge of the school grounds.

Luke turned away from the sky to look into Jade's face. "I'm really hoping you'll get on well in Sheffield, you know. I think it'll be great. I just wish I could be with you."

"And I wish I could be with you. You might need me to rescue you again and I won't be there."

"You can beam music to me through Malc, can't you?"

Jade smiled. "Yeah. I can send music, talk to you every day. I can send him pictures and he can project them onto a handy wall."

"Nice. But you won't be there. Not really."

"Pretend, Luke. Pretend."

Jade squeezed his hand and at once Luke shivered.

He remembered!

All those years ago, under the same sky, Kerryanne had taken his hand. That weak touch under the blanket had been his last contact with his little sister. By some strange instinct, his parents had known that the disease would steal their daughter on the following morning, so they were making her last night special.

Luke shivered. Tomorrow, he would lose something else. Tomorrow, something else would die, something inside him. He grasped Jade's hand and hung on tightly as if together they could hold back the dawn.

Want to find out how Luke Harding gets on in London? Here is the first chapter of the next brilliant **Traces** *story,* **Lost Bullet.** *Read on for a taste of more forensic crime-solving with Luke and Malc.*

TRACES: LOST BULLET

The white boy walking along Tottenham Court Corridor spotted a tree snake in the elder growing up the side of a house. He was about to move on, keeping away from it, when he was distracted by a small piece of paper that fluttered out of an upstairs window. Pushed along by the breeze, the notepaper sailed straight towards his head. Owen grabbed it in his fist as if he'd caught a moth that was threatening to land on his face. Immediately, there was a scream. "White scum!" It was so loud, so angry and high-pitched that Owen could not even tell if it had come from a man or woman. He wasn't going to hang around to find out who had shouted, because he recognized pure hatred in that voice. He shoved the piece of paper into his pocket and ran.

On either side of Owen, rampant ivy, elder and clematis were choking the buildings. The rifle poking ominously out of the window above and behind him was camouflaged by the masses of leaves. When Owen heard the first shot, he let out a frightened yelp and ducked. Covering his head with his hands would have been useless against the bullet if it had been on target, but it thudded into the trunk of the elm tree just to his right. Refusing to freeze with fear, he dashed away quickly. Weaving his way down the windy London corridor, swerving round the trees that had pushed their way up through the tarmac, he tried to make it difficult for the sniper to get a clear shot at him.

The second bullet ricocheted off the ground in front of him and to the left, but the third caught his hand. He cried out in pain but did not dare to stop. Cradling his injured left hand in his right, he stumbled on towards the junction. In a few seconds, he could turn into Oxford Freeway, safe from the person with an itchy finger on the trigger. As he dodged round another tree, a window shattered with the force of the next stray shot.

Once, before Owen was born, Oxford Freeway had been busy with automatic cabs, its walkway bustling with pedestrians. But no one had been employed to maintain it, or any of central London's routes, so nature had reclaimed lost territory. The cabs' on-board computers, equipped with the latest artificial intelligence, soon learned to avoid the centre of London because it became impossible to negotiate the erupting trees and shrubs. Besides, too many passengers and pedestrians were mugged in those parts to risk it.

Owen knew Oxford Freeway only as a concrete and wildlife jungle, the natural habitat of rats, snakes and

crooks. Still, until bullets learned how to turn corners, he could escape in the neglected freeway.

At the sound of another gunshot, two red squirrels darted up an old elm. At once, Owen felt his right foot give way as if someone had kicked it from under him. He gasped and faltered yet he experienced no pain. He expected to cry out in agony when he put his weight back on that leg but he felt only some extra pressure on his heel. The bullet had hit the tarmac, bounced up, thudded into the sole of his shoe and come to rest harmlessly in the thick layer of rubber.

Desperate to keep on his feet, Owen staggered to the junction with Oxford Freeway. Two small patches of ivy clawing up the nearest house exploded, revealing red brick underneath. Chest heaving, Owen darted round the corner where he was shielded from the rifle fire. Yet he did not relax or slow down. He scurried along the corridor, in case the sniper came out of hiding and tailed him. Avoiding the tangle of overgrown vegetation, he raced as fast as he could, still clutching his bleeding left hand, until he got to Wardour Walkway. Turning left into the narrow passage, he zigzagged through the warren of alleys to cheat anyone who might try to follow him.

The stiffening breeze pushed him through the jungle of Soho, along with masses of fallen brown leaves. He emerged on Haymarket and headed for Whitehall and the river. If he could pick a safe path over the crumbling

Westminster Bridge, he could admit himself to Thomas's Hospital and get his hand fixed. The hospital had a reputation for not asking too many awkward questions before offering treatment. Owen glanced nervously behind him but the place was nearly deserted. Of course, it wasn't really deserted. It was just that, for their own protection, many people stayed behind locked doors – or at least out of sight. Anyway, Owen couldn't see anyone carrying a rifle. He dropped to walking pace, limping slightly because of the lump of metal embedded in the heel of his shoe, and made his way towards the Thames.

On the riverside, a group of people had hijacked a narrow cargo boat that should have been cruising sedately through the city, programmed to ignore London and deliver its load to the heart of England. The goods on this particular auto-barge would feed and clothe London bandits, not the plush Midlands. Picking his way carefully across the run down bridge, Owen looked down on the thieves shouting to each other below him on the south bank. One lad stood out from the rest because he was completely bald. No doubt the bandits would have time to empty the boat because The Authorities were never in a hurry to deal with petty theft in London.

There was a burning sensation in Owen's left palm. As far as he could tell, the bullet had gone straight

through the fleshy part between his thumb and forefinger. Like everyone else who ventured into central London, Owen had been injured a few times but he had never been shot before. It was a new and hurtful experience. It had taken him by surprise also because he had become skilled at avoiding crime, especially muggings, on London corridors.

Those outbursts of violence were often caused by people who were scared witless by London's reputation. When they went out, they armed themselves with a hefty piece of metal or wood for self-defence. Whenever they confronted another person, they got their attack in first because they thought they'd be too late if they waited until they'd figured out whether they were in danger or not.

Conventional firearms were popular for sport, but in the corridors they were not common. The stinger – an electric stun gun – had become the bandits' weapon of choice. The person on the other end of that rifle wasn't a traditional mugger. It could just have been someone insanely protective of a property but Owen had never been targeted in Tottenham Court Corridor before. It could have been someone who had decided to take pot-shots at passers-by for fun but the taunt about the colour of his skin made Owen believe that he'd been singled out.

Waiting in a hospital cubicle, encircled by flimsy curtains, Owen dug the scrap of plain white paper out of his pocket and held it in his right hand. Someone had written '72 Russell Plaza', in blue ink, on a page from a notepad. That was it. Nothing else. There wasn't even anything on the other side. Owen shrugged and, when Dr Suleman entered, he slipped the note back into his pocket without another thought.

The doctor turned her nose up at the sight of her patient. "Oh dear," she muttered.

Owen was not sure whether the medic was referring to his injury, his genetically flawed skin or his rough appearance. For a second he thought that he saw disapproval in Dr Suleman's eyes. At least it wasn't the prejudice of the person who had hoped to bury a bullet in Owen's heart or head, rather than his hand and heel. Owen held up his blood-encrusted hand and said, "It's a bullet wound."

"Oh dear," Dr Suleman repeated. Gingerly, perhaps even reluctantly, she examined the damaged palm but did not query why Owen had been shot. "It looks worse than it is." Talking to a hidden computer, she called for a scan and then watched a three-dimensional skeletal image form in the air just in front of her. She walked around the hologram, studying the wound carefully from all angles, and then announced, "You're lucky."

"I am?"

"It could've been worse. The bullet's nicked a bone but it'll heal on its own. I can give you a local

anaesthetic, clean it up, and sew it back together. You'll be fine." She paused before adding, "I don't suppose you've got an identity card, have you?"

"Do I need one? Not sure where mine is."

The doctor shook her head like an instructor confronting a hopeless pupil. "Never mind," she said as if she'd rather report him to The Authorities.

In Owen's mind, her tone confirmed it. The doctor disliked his lifestyle rather than his colour. "Thanks," he said, ignoring her disquiet.

While she worked on the wound, Dr Suleman asked Owen where he had been attacked. "Tottenham Court? I'll watch that on the way home."

"Don't think you'll have the same problem," Owen replied.

"Why's that?"

"Likely it was a brown supremacy thing."

The doctor nodded knowingly but said nothing.

Owen decided to leave the spent bullet in the sole of his shoe where it would be his secret memento of a daring escape from a crazed sniper. With a bandaged and throbbing hand, he walked away from Thomas's Hospital. Just along the bank, the bandits were still emptying the barge that they had commandeered. The blustery wind was threatening to develop into a full-scale storm. Glancing up at the bad-tempered clouds that were gathering in the dark sky, Owen grimaced. It was time to find shelter.

Once, Anna Suleman used to flash her identity card past the freeway reader, state her home address and then jump into a cab. As soon as she was seated, the computerized cab would take off along Westminster, over the bridge and seek out a passable route on the corridors running north. Now, it was useless to call for one. She hadn't seen a vehicle between the hospital and her home near Regent's Common for years. Instead, she walked. If her partner was working the same shifts, they would walk together. Now that cabs shunned the place, they had a choice of paths. They could keep to the proper walkways, they could use the large freeways that had both walkways and corridors, or they could trudge along the disused corridors where walking used to be forbidden because of the danger from high-speed cabs.

Today, after her shift at Thomas's Hospital, Dr Suleman stepped out into the dusk alone and was drenched almost immediately. The November downpour had begun in style. The thirsty vegetation relished the driving rainfall, but Anna cursed. As she made for the bridge, she blinked over and over again to try to keep her vision clear and to stop the wind and raindrops stinging her tired eyes. All that she could see, though, was mist. There was perhaps something to her left, a sudden movement like a shifting shadow, but then it was gone. Perhaps it was a trick of the storm.

It was hopeless. She could not walk through this weather. She spun round and headed back for the hospital entrance. It was then that the shape returned – definitely this time. It was a figure, striding towards her, holding. . . something. Anna screwed up her eyes but it was like trying to see a bat flying across the night sky. "Is anybody there?"

The slippery figure had vanished again. There was nothing but the ferocious sound of the squally cloudburst. The nearest lamp was flickering on and off. Probably, water was getting inside it and playing havoc with the electrical contacts. The rest of the lights were battling to keep night at bay but succeeded only in illuminating countless raindrops.

"Alex? Is that you?" Anna called.

This time there was an answer. "Are you a doctor?"

Dr Suleman stopped and shouted in the direction of the voice, "Yes. Are you hurt?" She wiped her eyes. "Where are you? What do you want?"

Lightning punctured the air. Anna heard one more word before the thunder deafened her. "Respect!" Through the deluge, she could barely see the person who had spoken. She certainly didn't see the rifle. Engulfed by nature's fierce roar, she could not distinguish between the brutal blast of the weapon and the explosion of the storm.